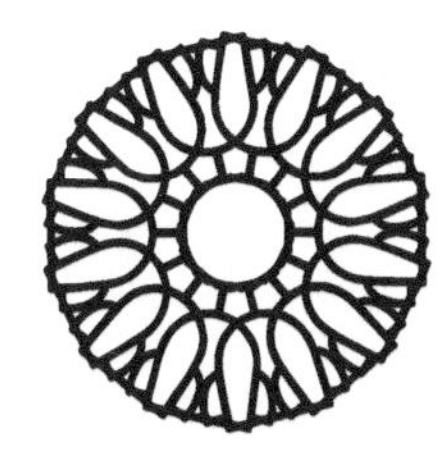

MOON PRINCESSES AND SPACE MONSTERS

COLORING BOOK

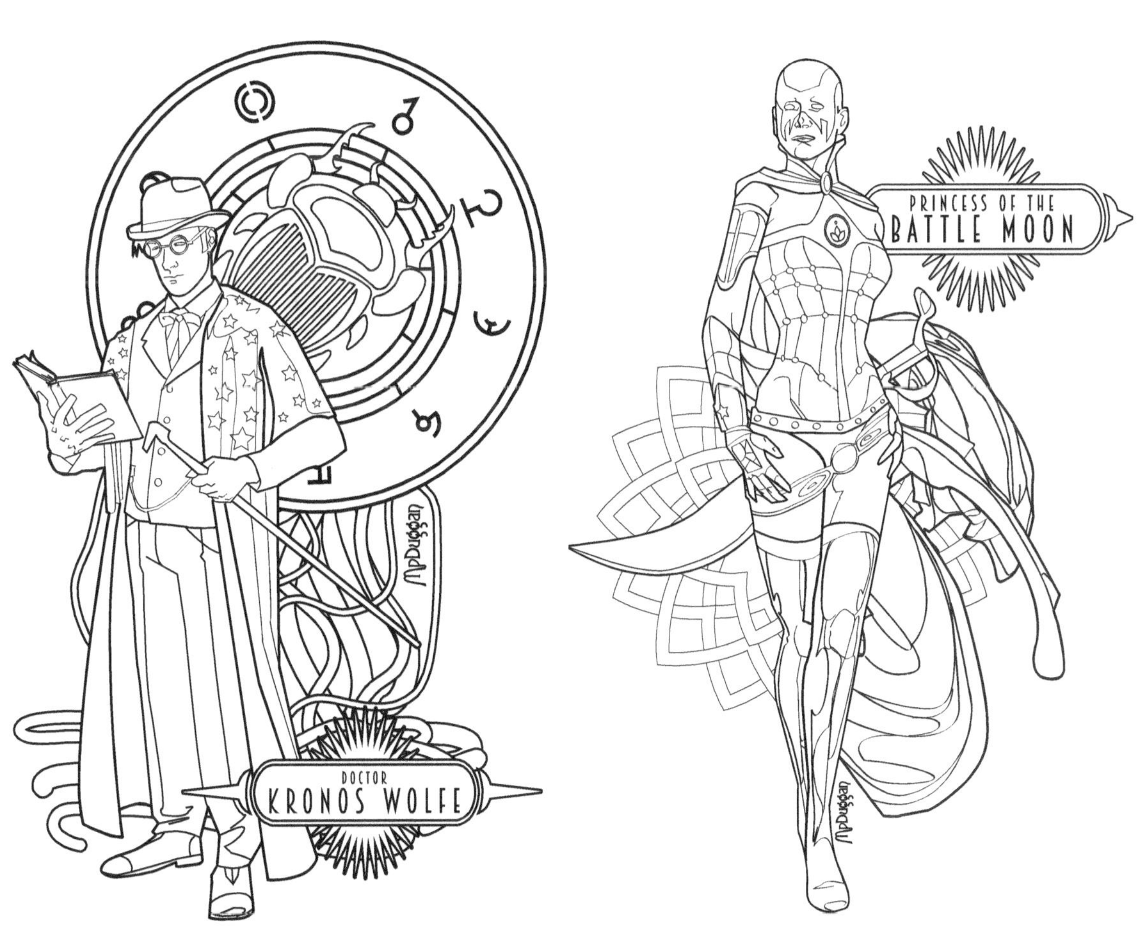

WRITTEN AND ILLUSTRATED BY M. PATRICK DUGGAN

Copyright © 2017 M. Patrick Duggan
All Rights Reserved.

No part of this book may be reproduced or transmitted in any form or by any means, electronic, or mechanical, including photocopying, recording, or by any information storage retrieval system, without written permission from the publisher, except where permitted by law.

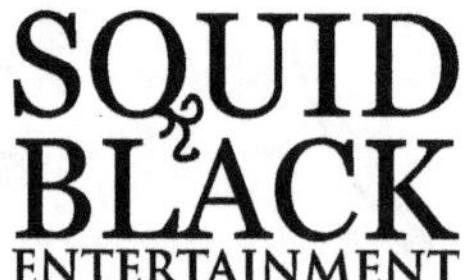

Published by Squid Black Entertainment
squidblack.com

Printed in the United States of America

10 9 8 7 6 5 4 3 2 1

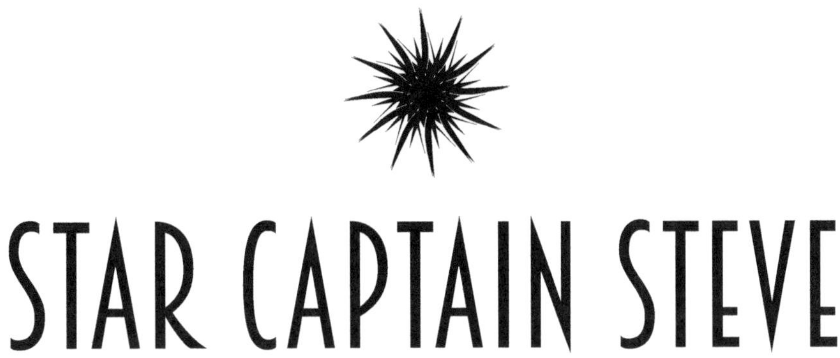

STAR CAPTAIN STEVE

HERO

Blown off-course by solar winds, Star Captain Steve crash-lands on a mysterious planet ruled by the Evil Galactic Emperor. He quickly discovers the lighter gravity of this new world gives him remarkable strength, and sets about making alliances with the forces of good who fight a constant war against evil.

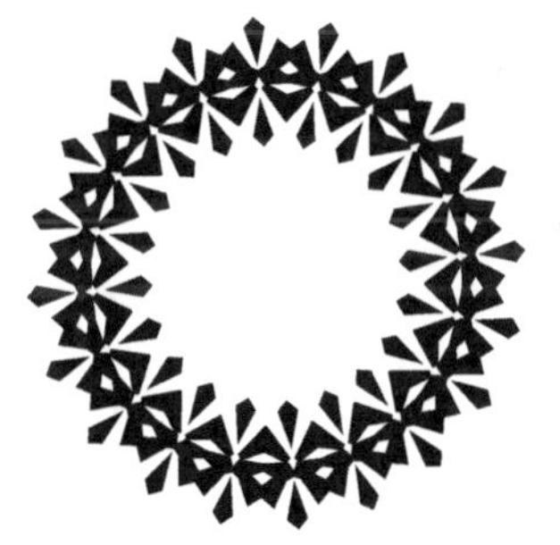

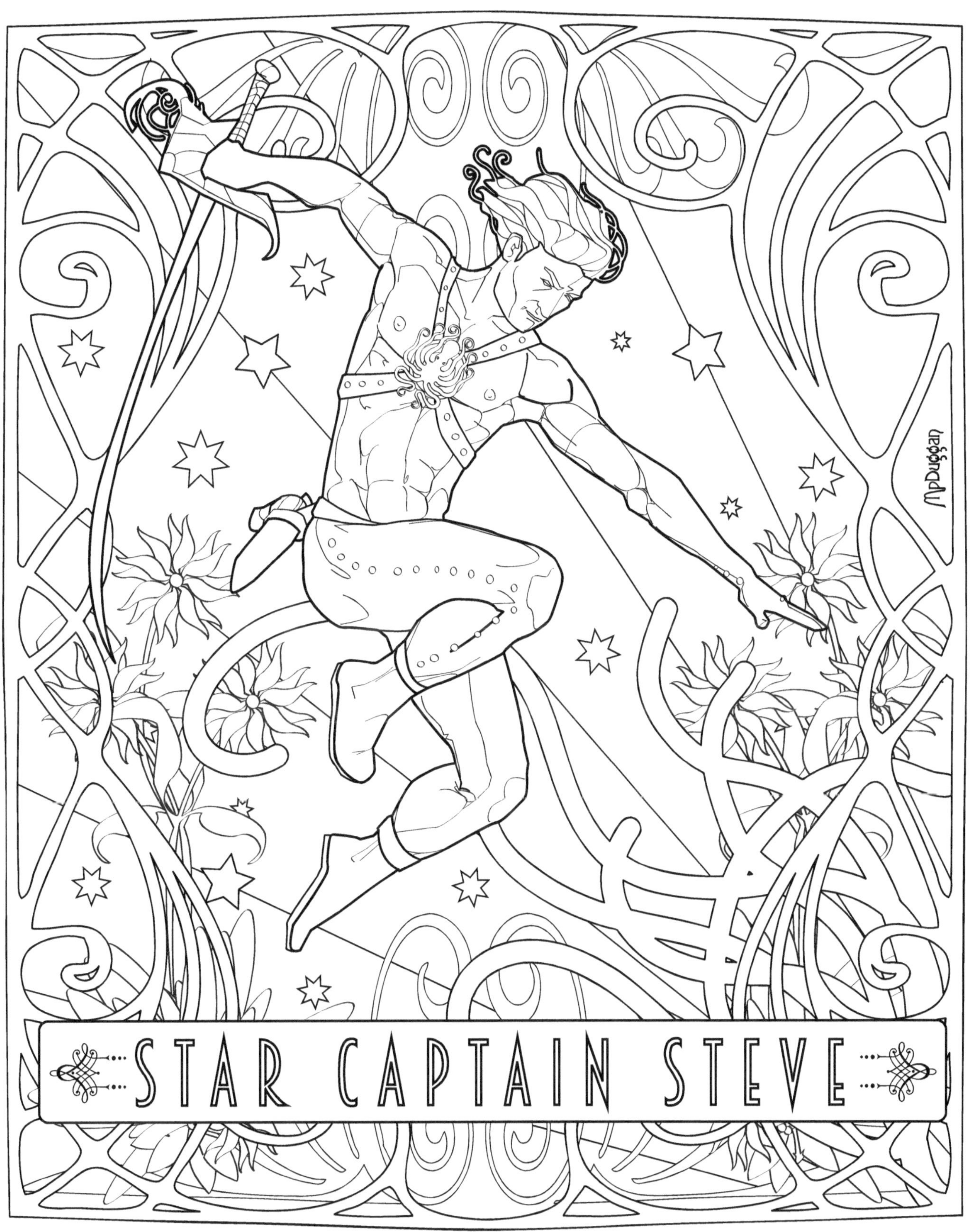
STAR CAPTAIN STEVE

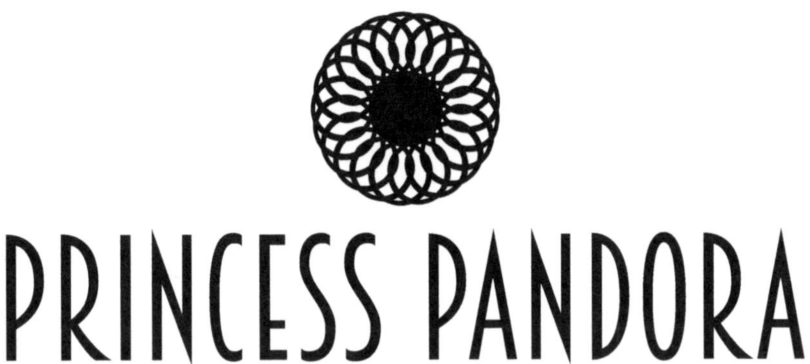

PRINCESS PANDORA

RULER OF THE MOON OF TITANIA

Ruler of one of the many moons circling the mysterious world, Pandora is a leader in the rebellion against the Evil Emperor.

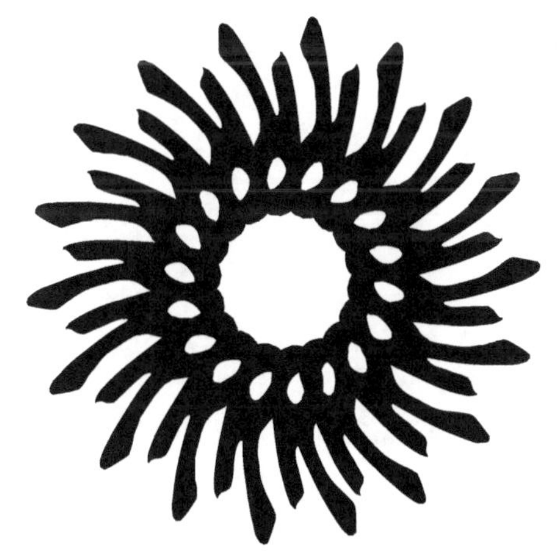

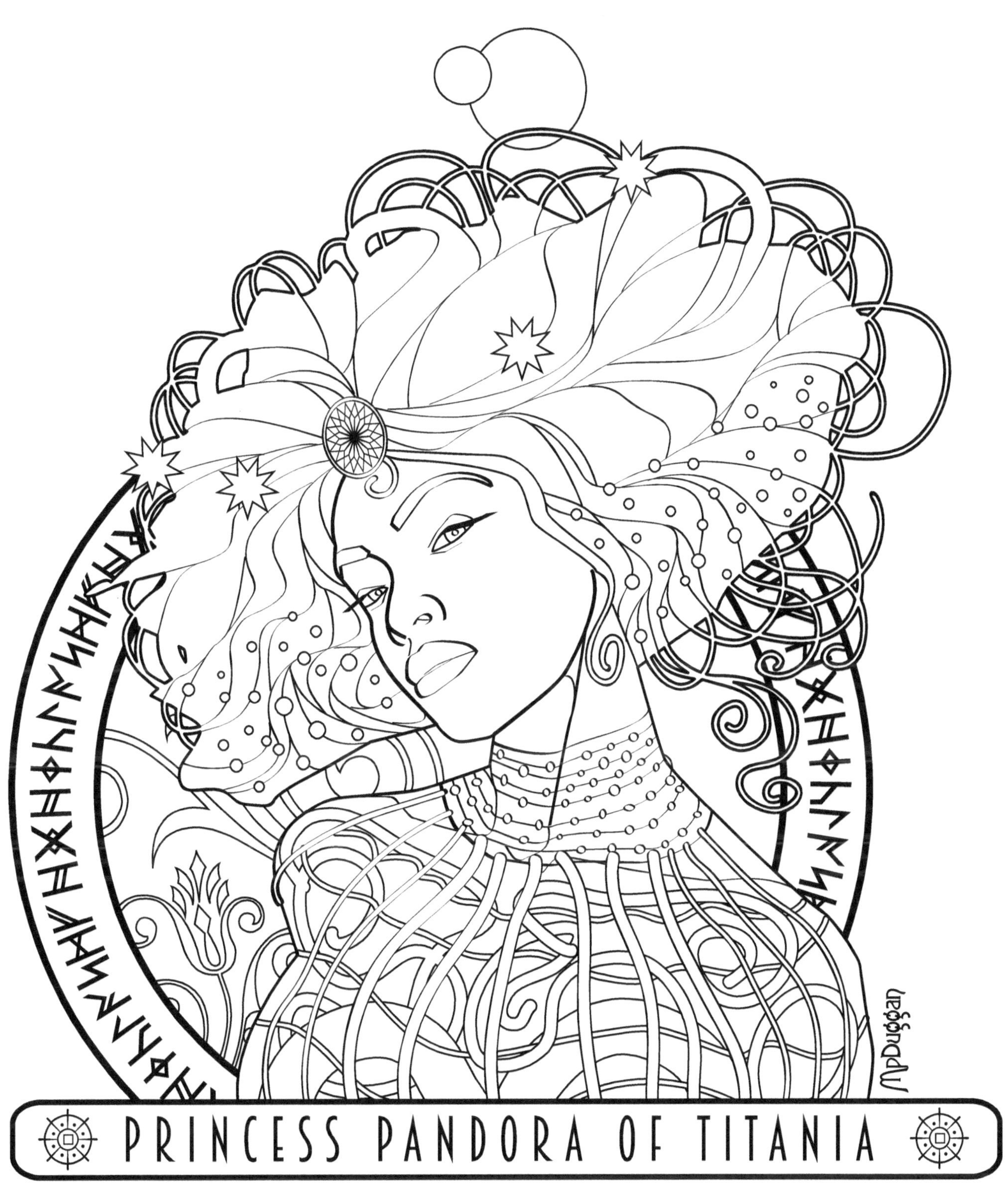
PRINCESS PANDORA OF TITANIA

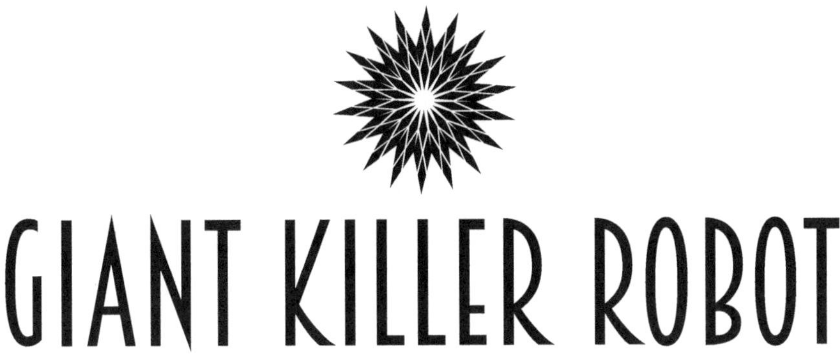

GIANT KILLER ROBOT

A DEADLY PROBLEM FOR EVERYONE

The Evil Galactic Emperor has a whole army of giant killer robots.

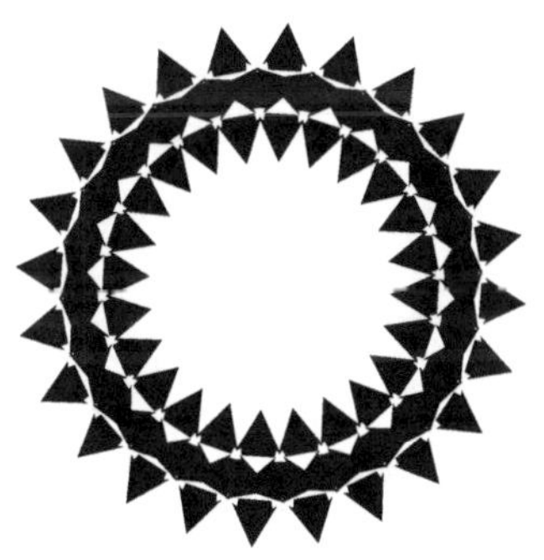

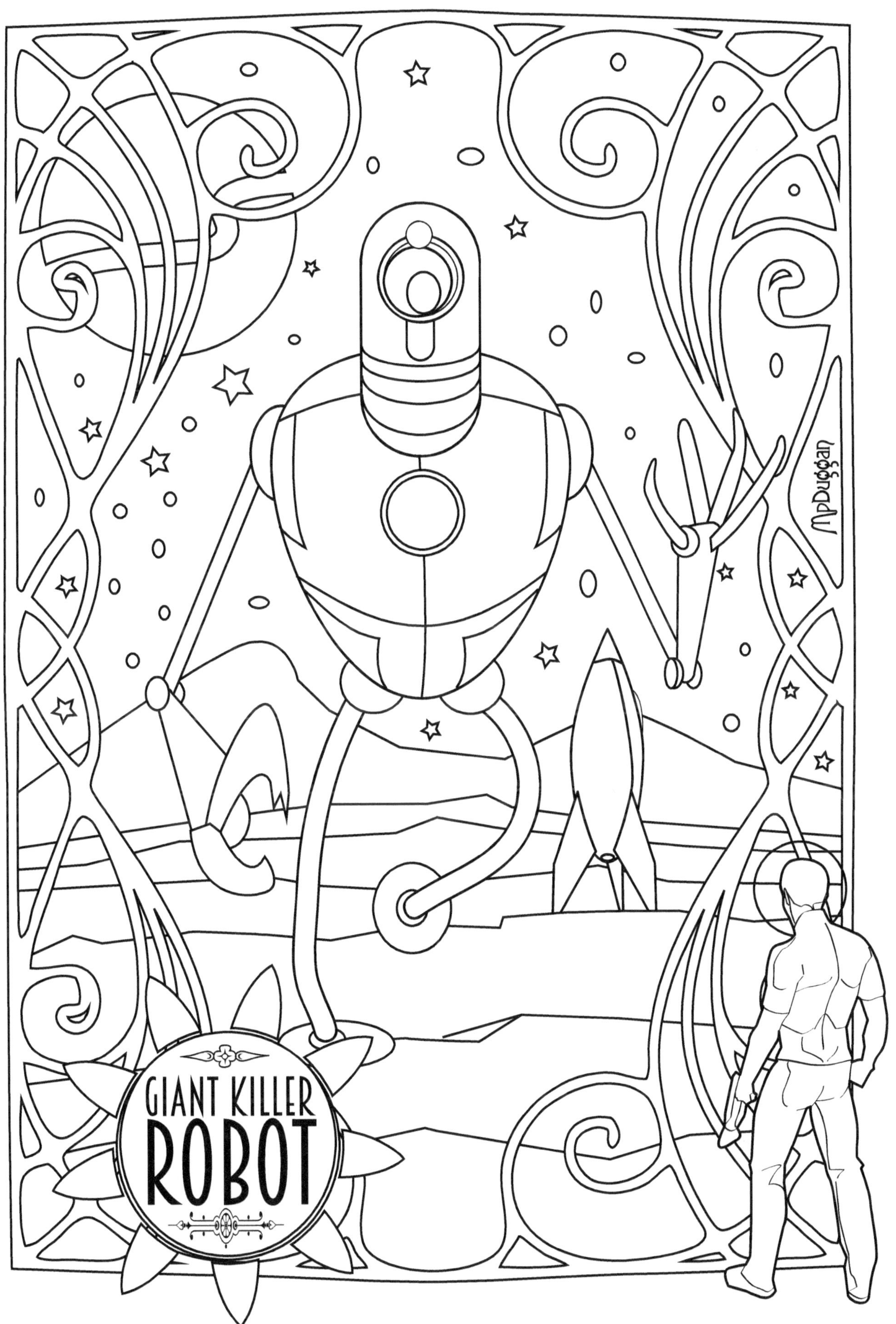
GIANT KILLER
ROBOT
MrDuggan 33

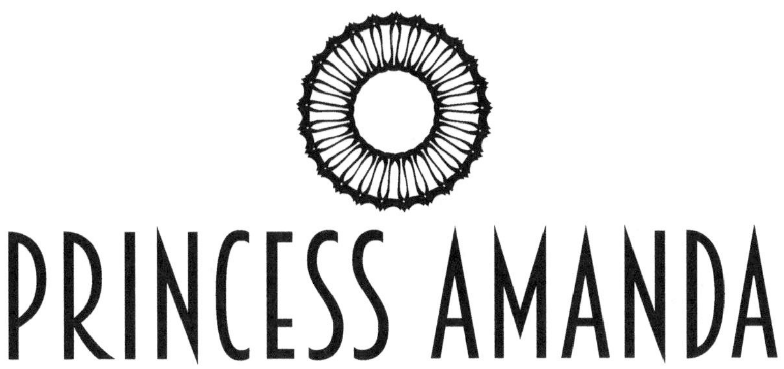

PRINCESS AMANDA

THE HIDDEN PRINCESS

Close ally to Princess Pandora is her fellow Moon Princess, Amanda, who went into hiding. But Amanda isn't quiet or invisible. She and her forces fight as guerillas against the forces of evil.

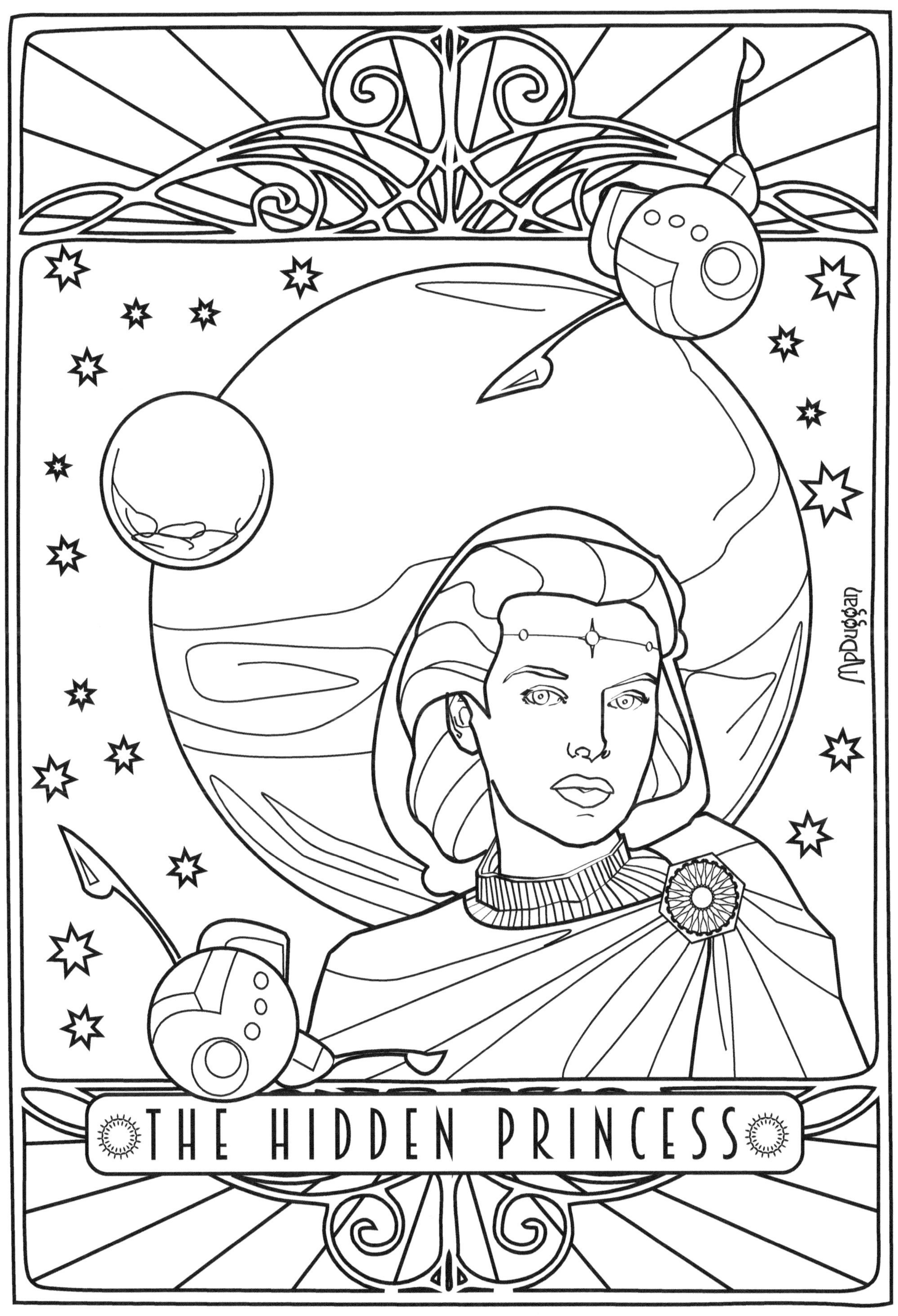
THE HIDDEN PRINCESS

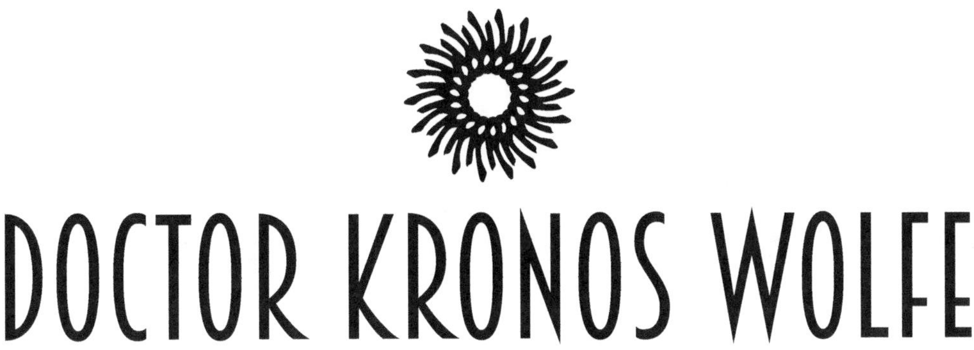

DOCTOR KRONOS WOLFE

BRILLIANT GENIUS

While adventuring on the myterious world, Star Captain Steve meets another human: Doctor Kronos Wolfe! But is the doctor really human... or something else? It is a great mystery, and perhaps we will never know. In the meantime, they become friends and the doctor helps in the battle against evil.

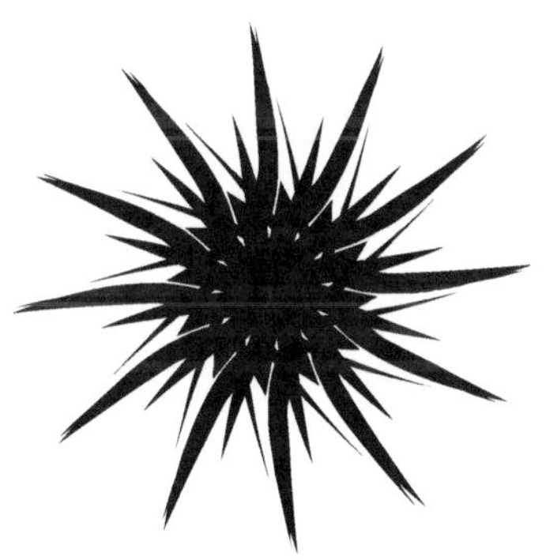

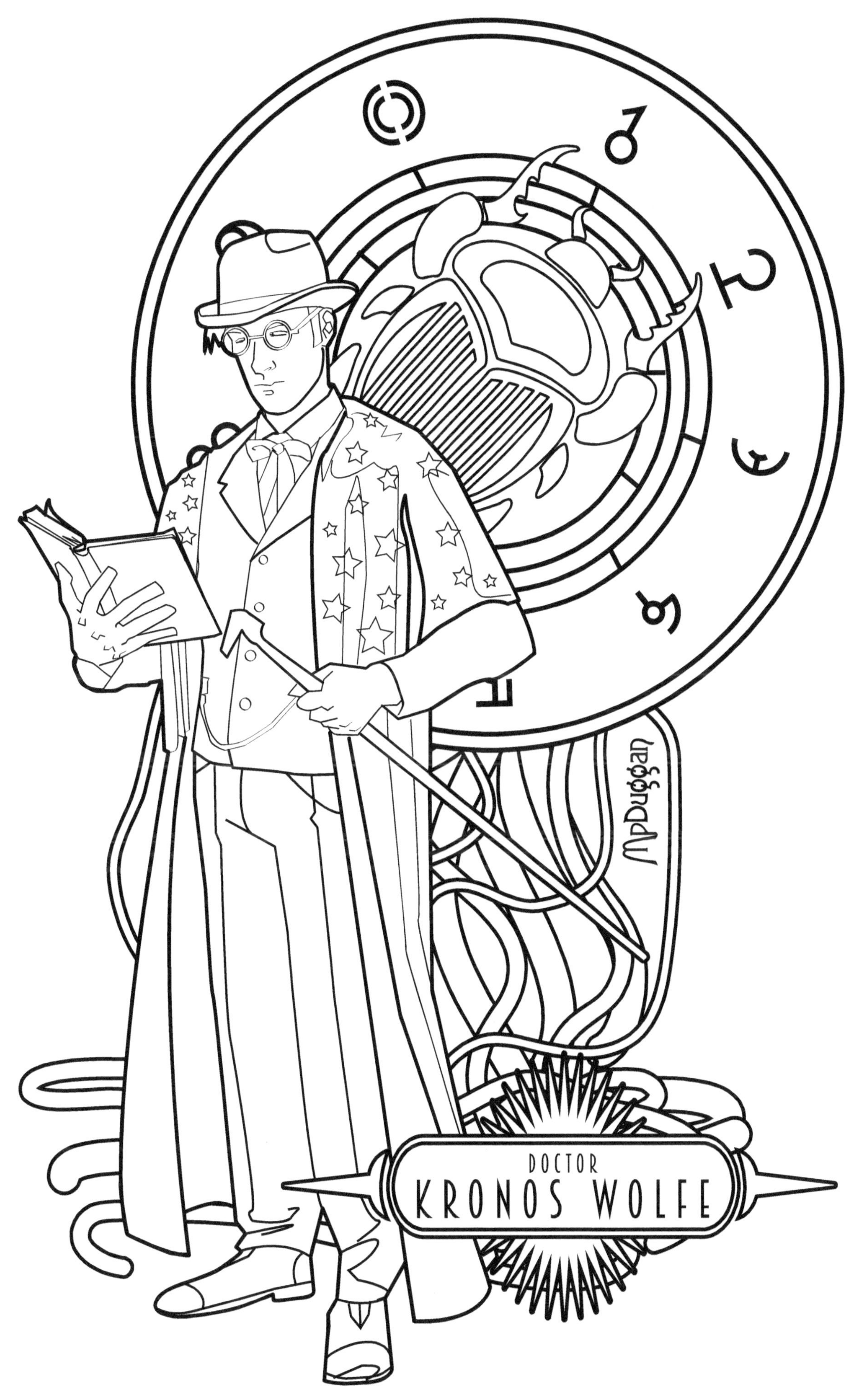
DOCTOR
KRONOS WOLFE
MpDuggan

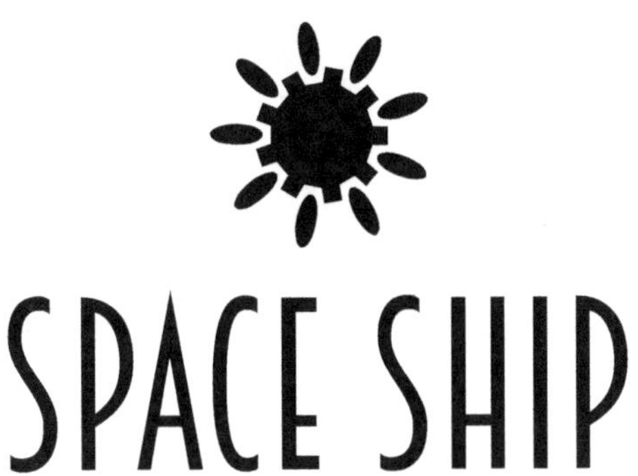

SPACE SHIP

A USEFUL DEVICE

Doctor Kronos Wolfe has his own space ship, which allows our heroes to seek allies across the solar system in the fight against evil!

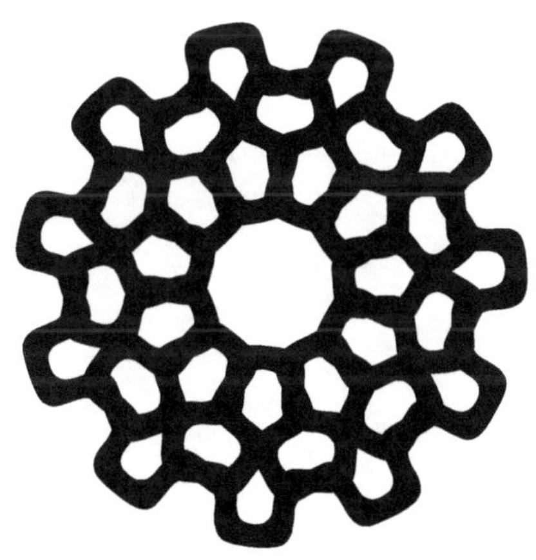

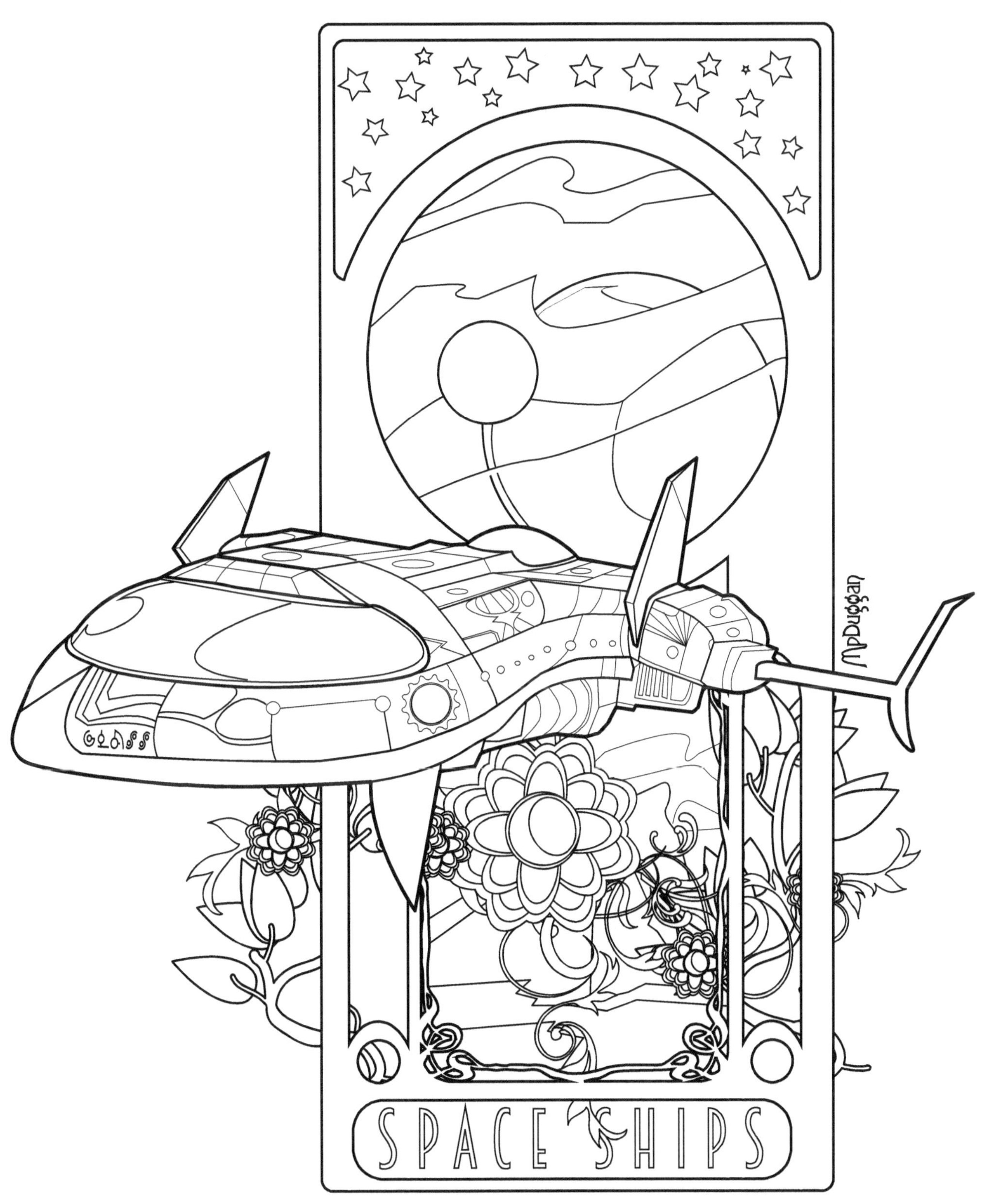
SPACE SHIPS

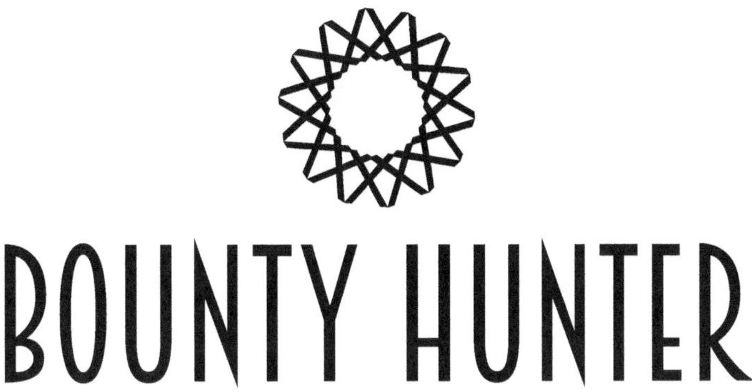

BOUNTY HUNTER

ANOTHER PROBLEM

Unfortunately, the Evil Galactic Emperor knows about Star Captain Steve,
so he hires an interstellar bounty hunter to track him down.
In addition to being very dangerous, she is rather beautiful.

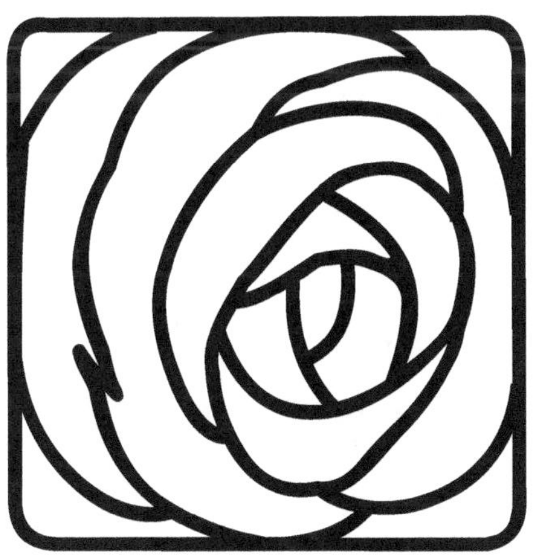

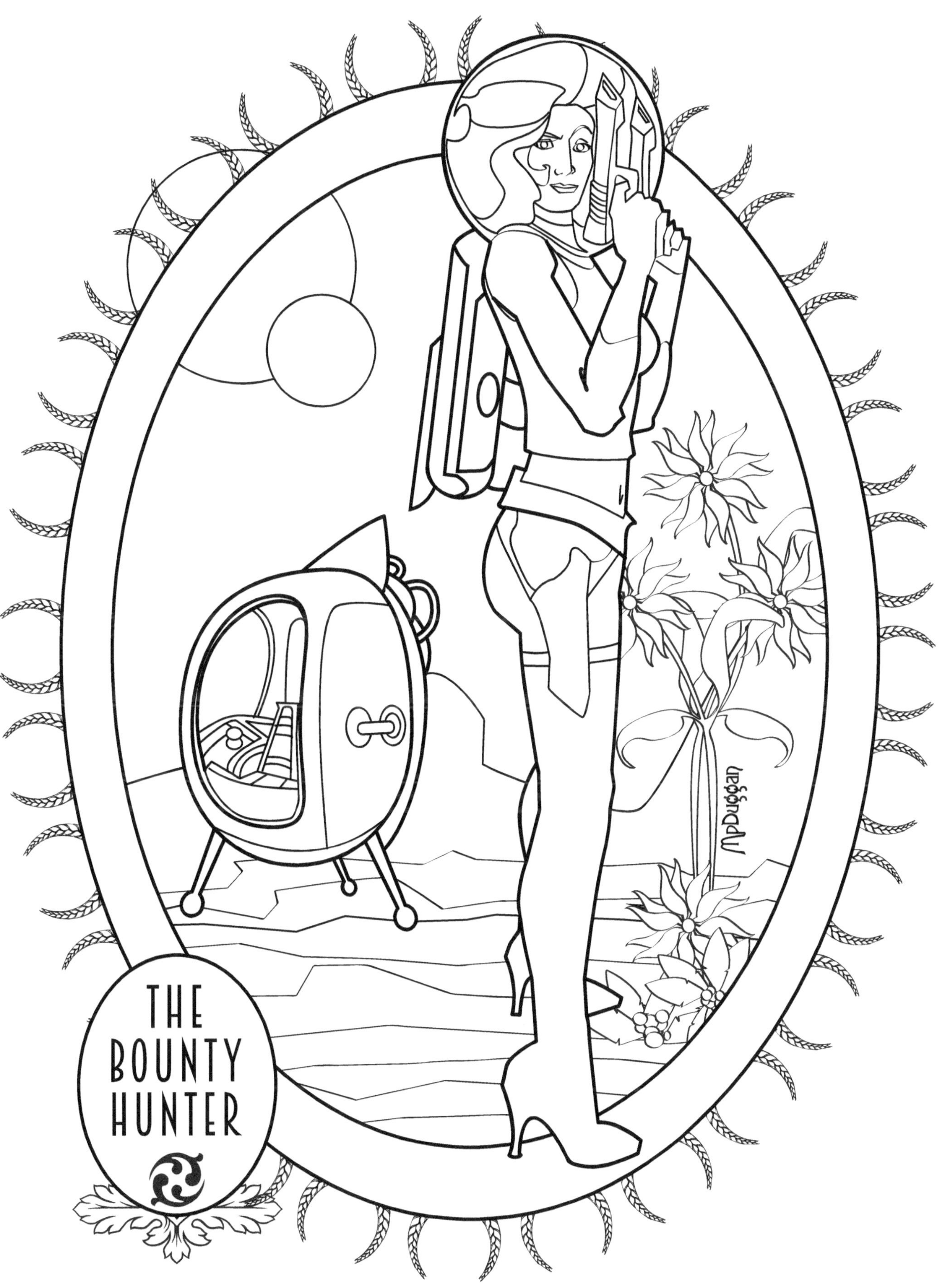
THE
BOUNTY
HUNTER
MpDuggan

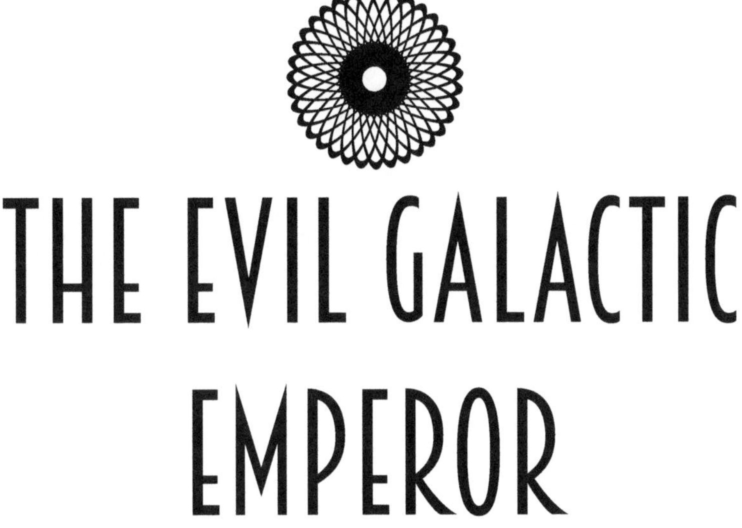

THE EVIL GALACTIC EMPEROR

THE FACE OF EVIL

Crafty, wicked, and completely evil--the Galactic Emperor is the worst of the worst!

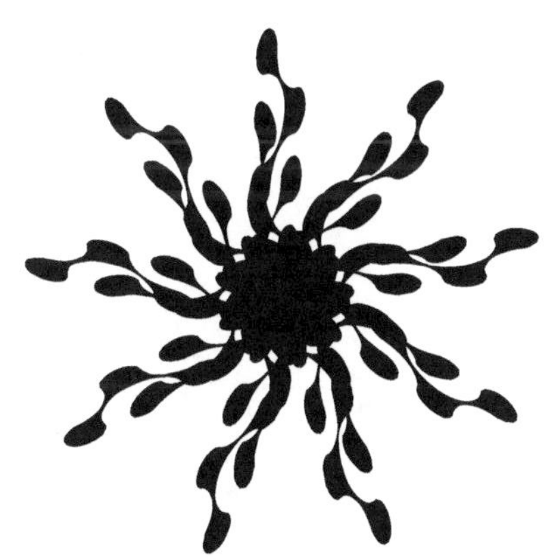

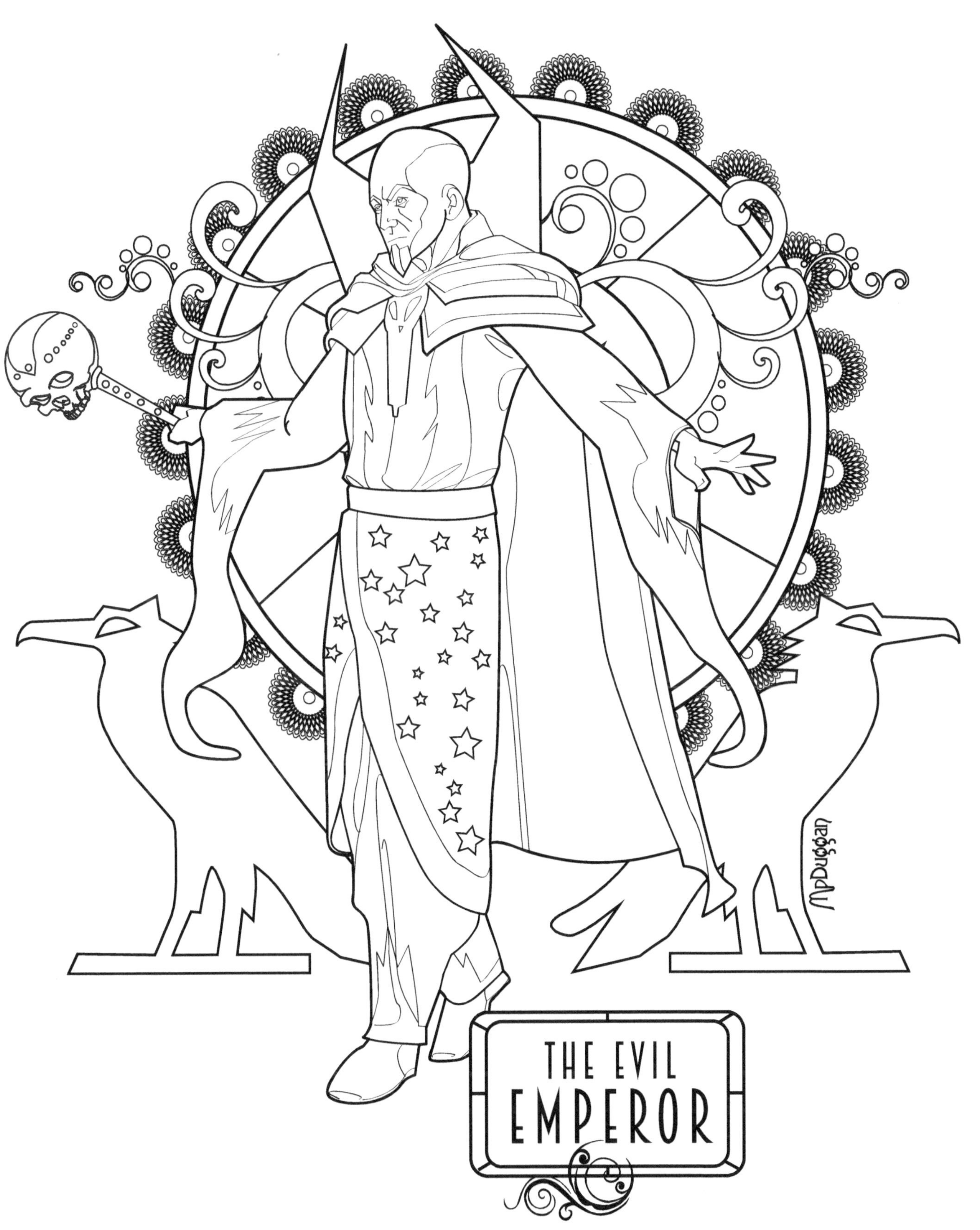
THE EVIL
EMPEROR

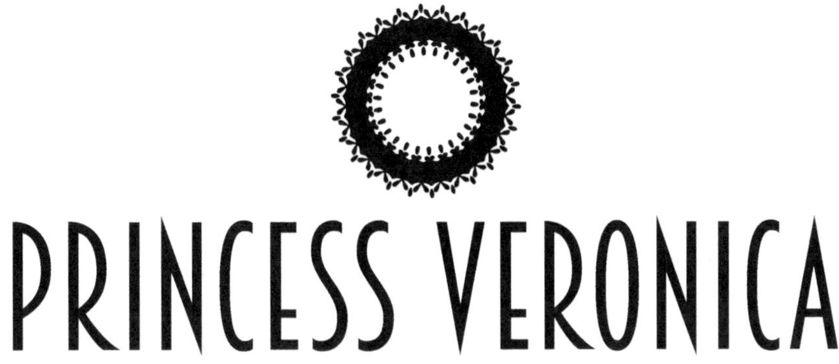

PRINCESS VERONICA

KEEPER OF SECRETS AND RULER OF THE MOON OF HYPERION

Fortunately, our heroes have more friends than they realize.
Princess Veronica's world is the repository of all knowledge in this part of the galaxy, so she stays informed and works to help the forces of good.

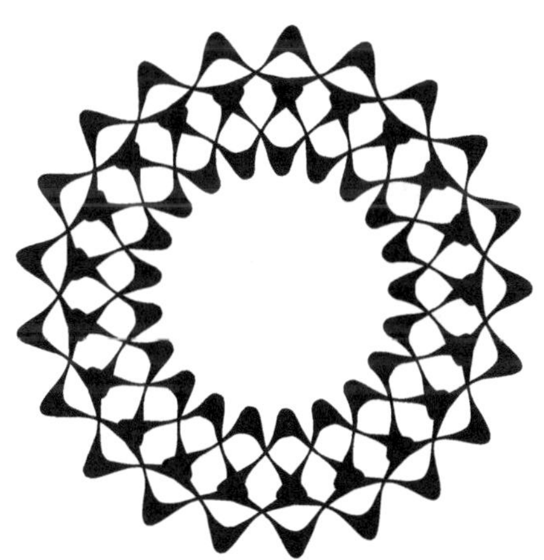

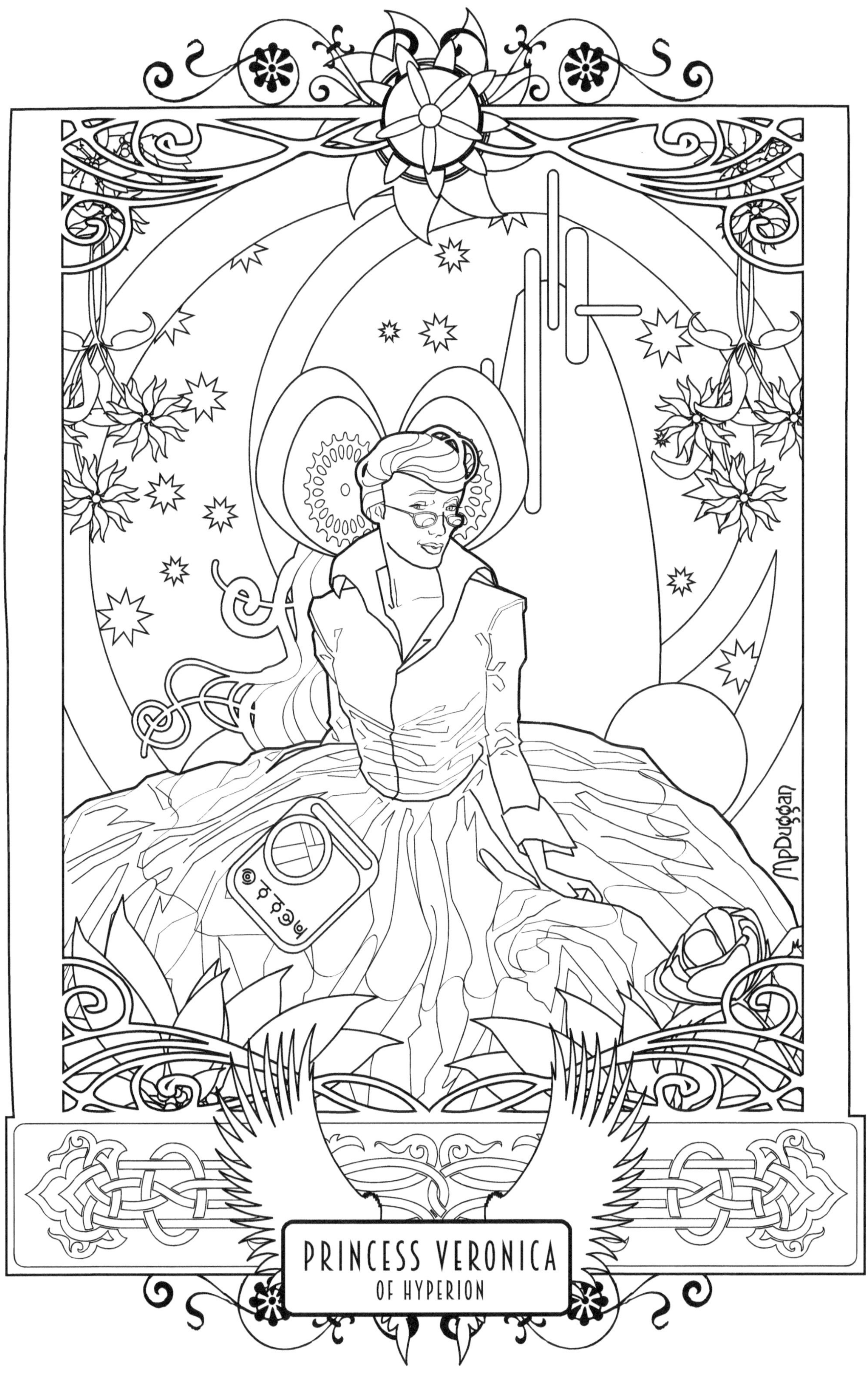
PRINCESS VERONICA
OF HYPERION

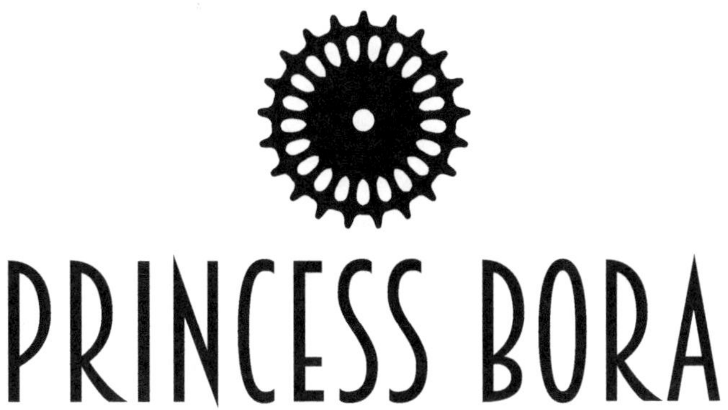

PRINCESS BORA

AN UNLIKELY FRIEND

At first, she was planning to kidnap Star Captain Steve and force him to father a race of superhuman soldiers. But then Princess Bora learned that the Evil Emperor had kidnapped her sister and imprisoned her in a pod, so she decided it would be better to rid the world of evil.

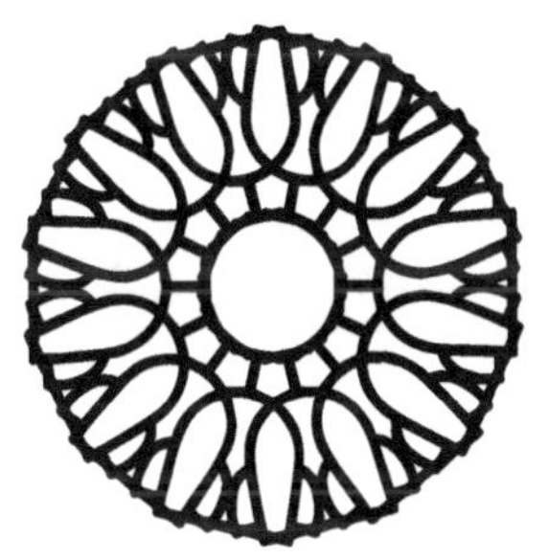

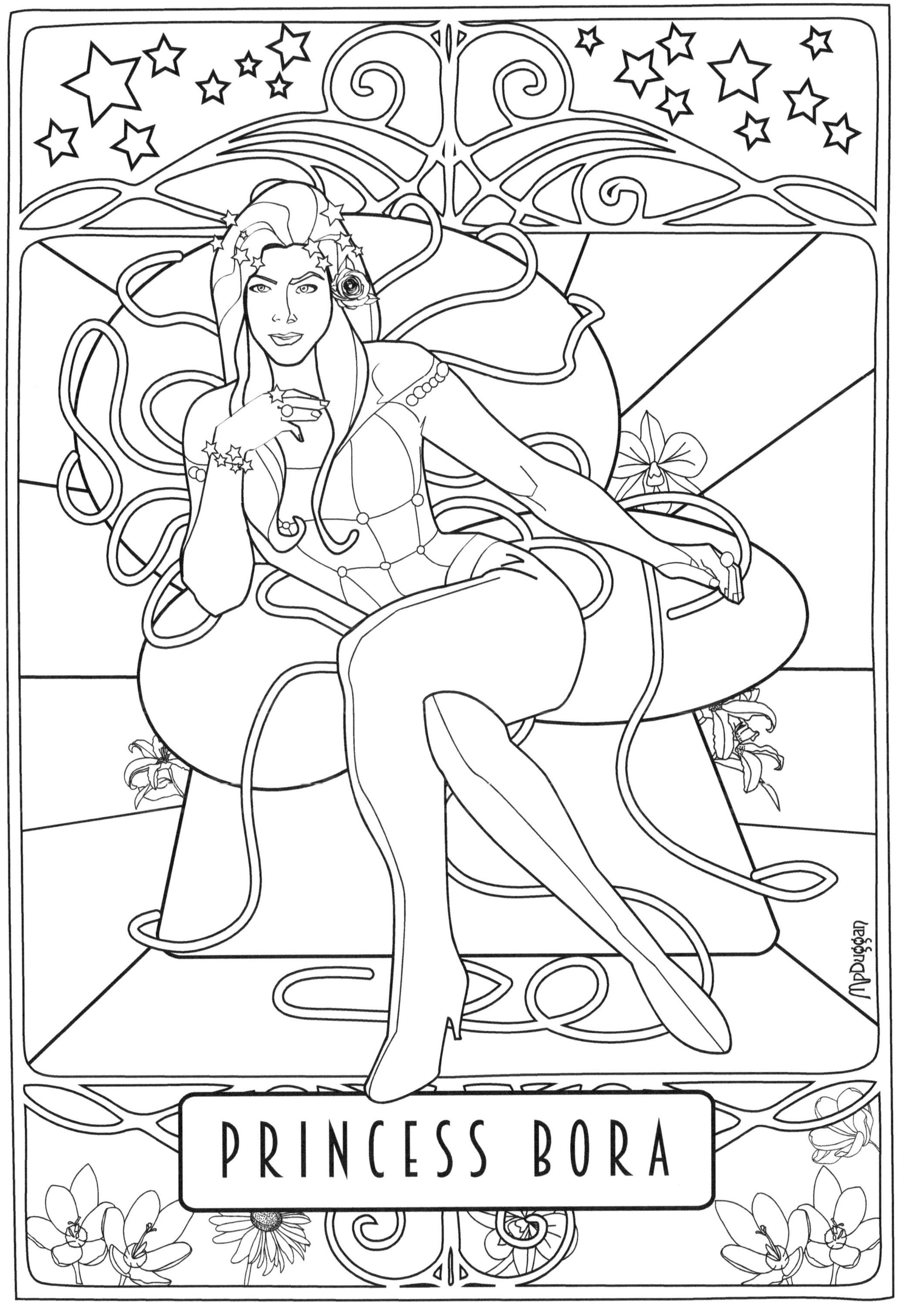
PRINCESS BORA

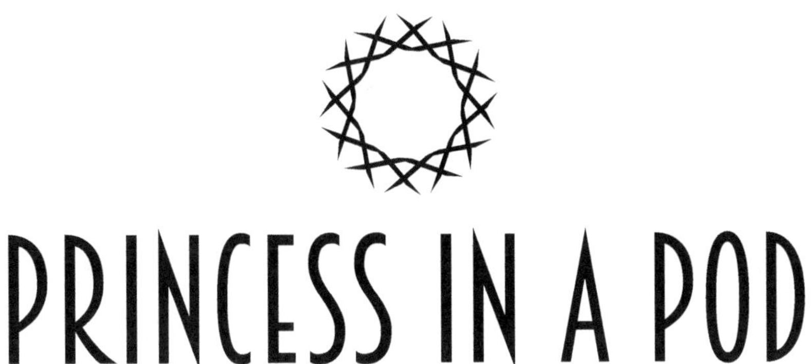

PRINCESS IN A POD

CAPTIVE MOON PRINCESS

Wrong place and the wrong time for this one. Fortunately, her sacrifice doesn't go unnoticed!

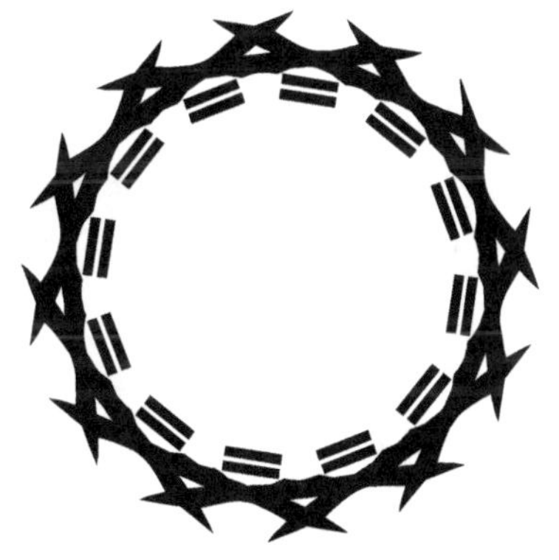

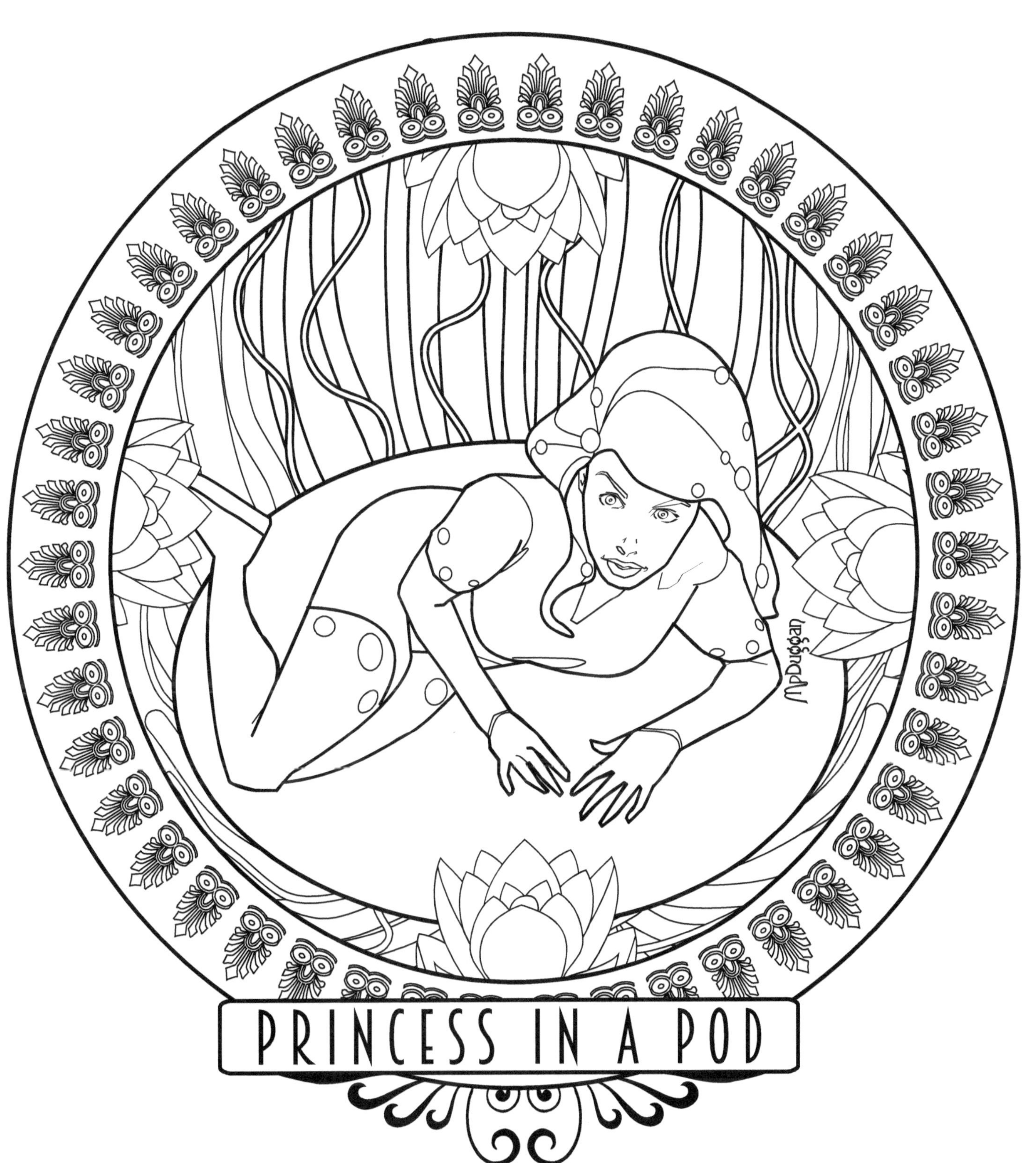
PRINCESS IN A POD

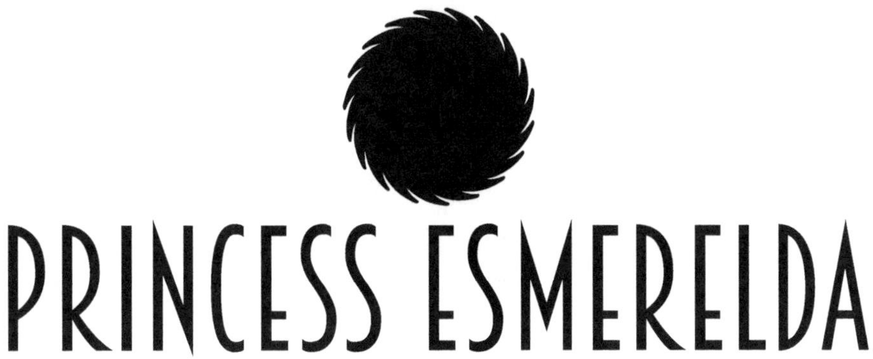

PRINCESS ESMERELDA

TECHNOCRATIC MOON PRINCESS

Originally, Princess Esmerelda was planning to stay neutral and see what happens.
But her cousin, Princess Veronica, manages to convince her to take a side.

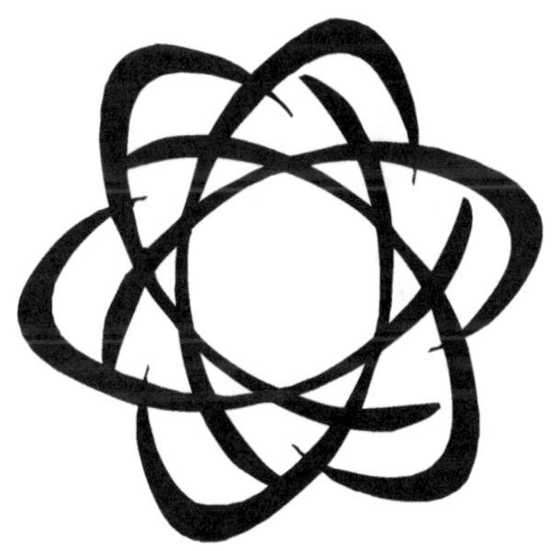

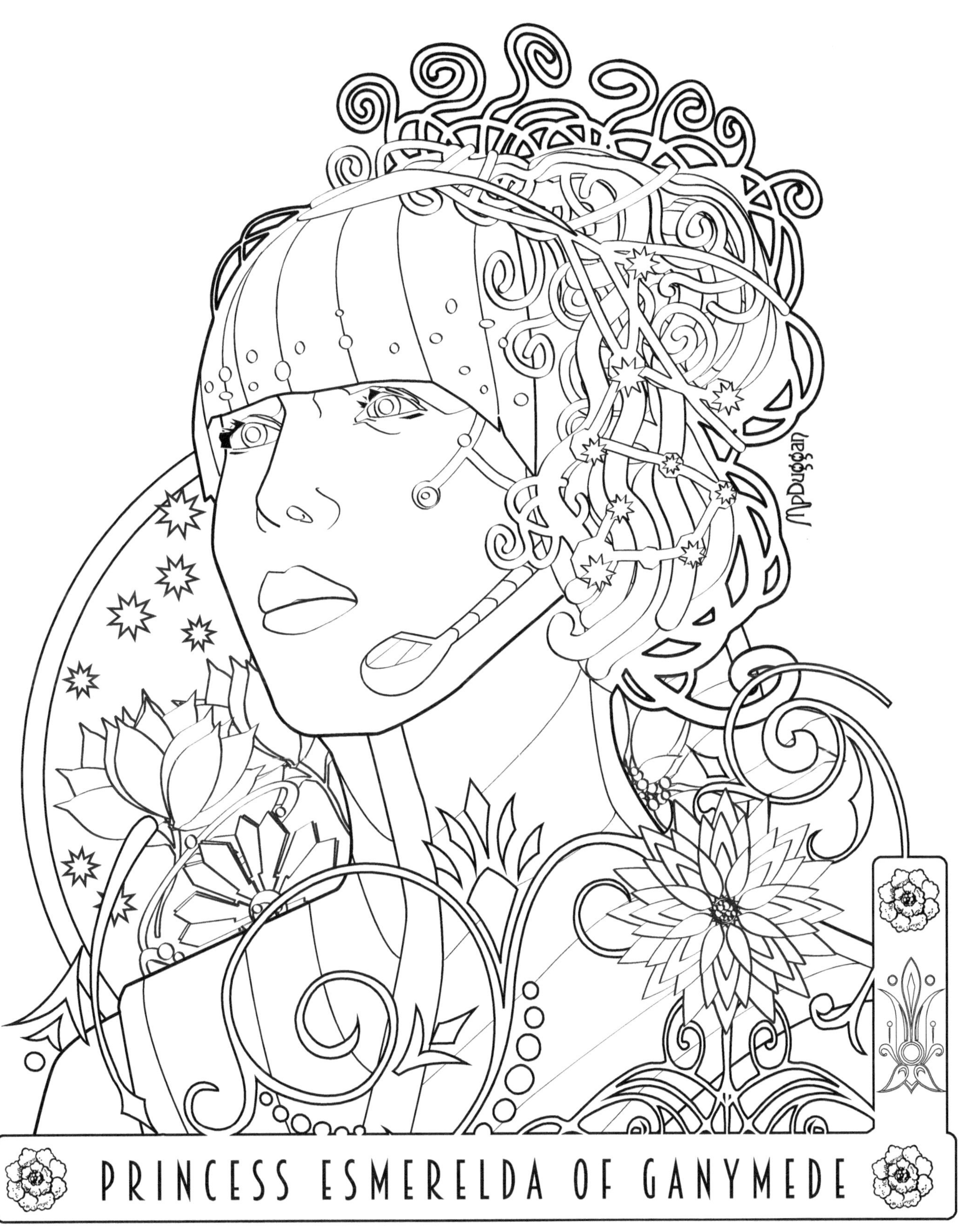
PRINCESS ESMERELDA OF GANYMEDE

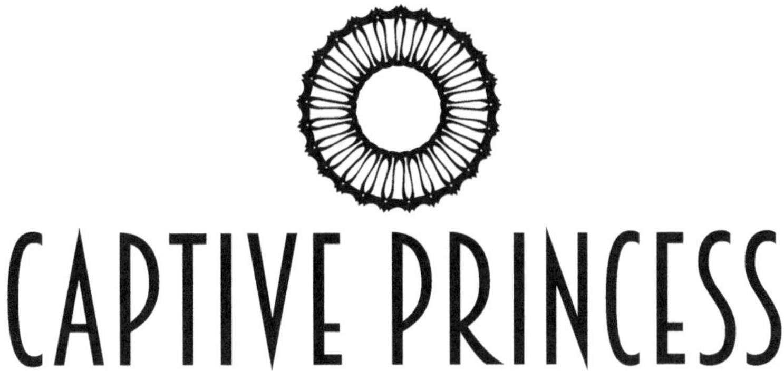

CAPTIVE PRINCESS

UNFORTUNATE BYSTANDER

Another Moon Princess held against her will. Will evil never stop?

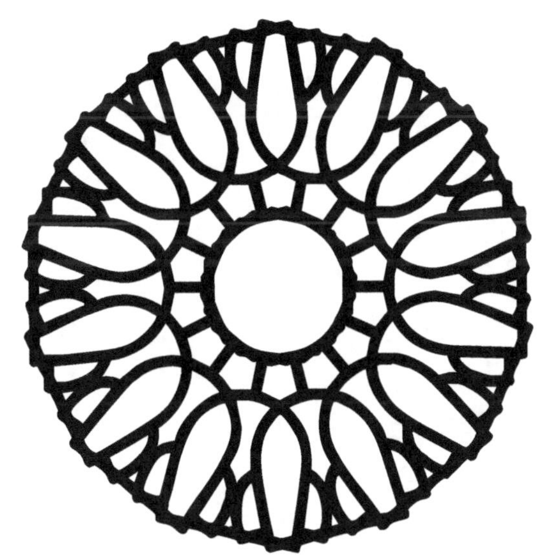

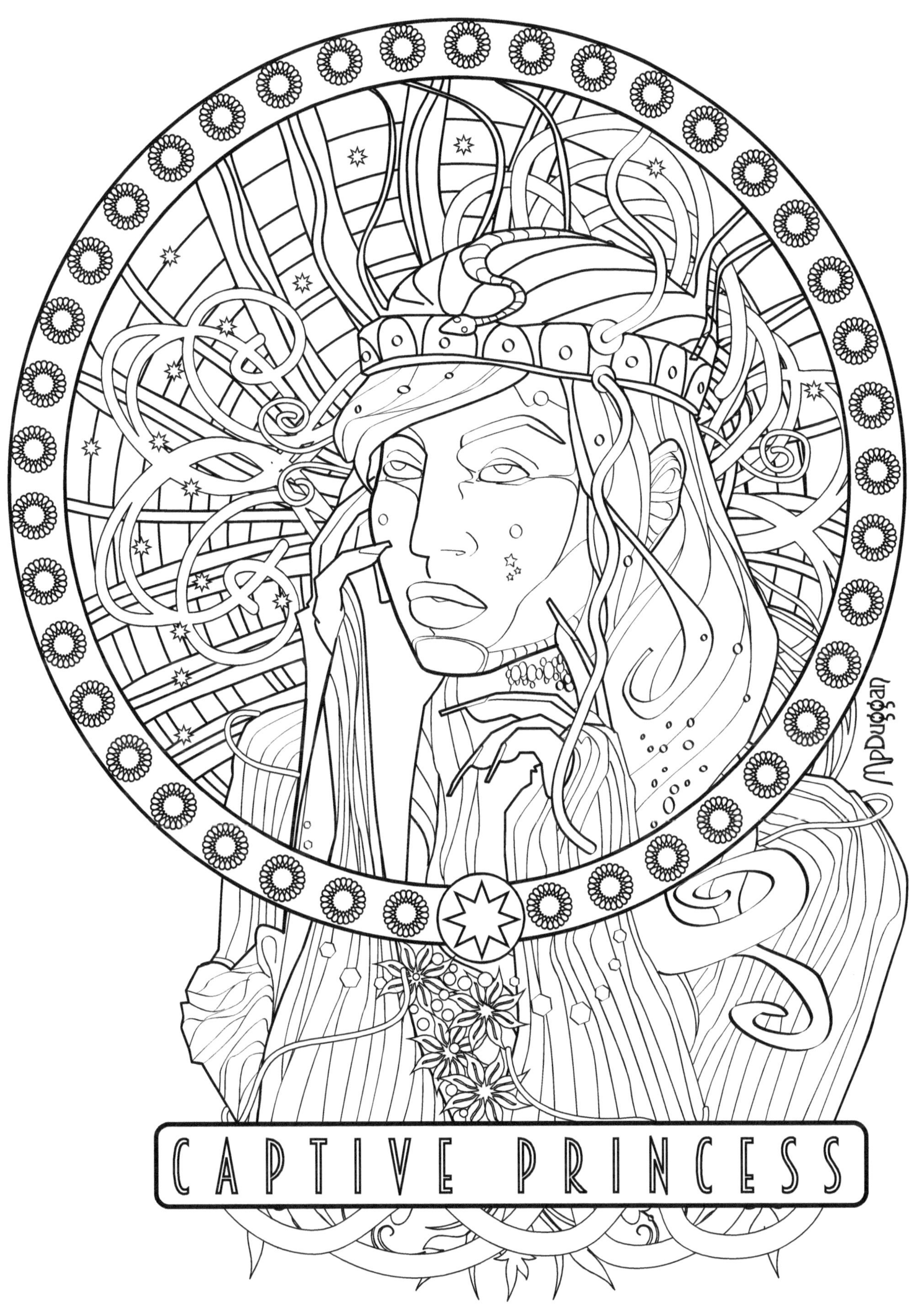
CAPTIVE PRINCESS

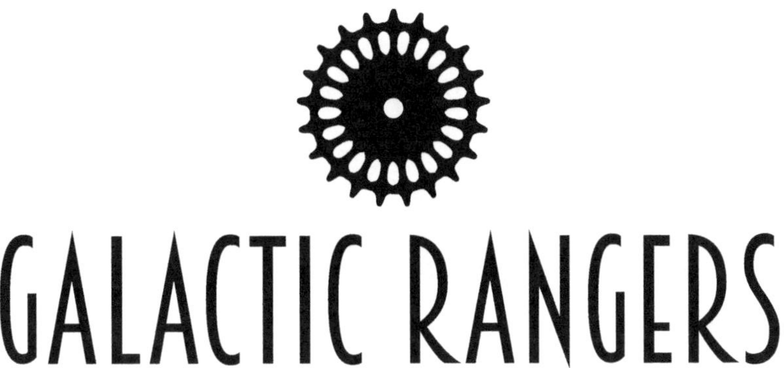

ALLIES FROM AFAR

Just as things are looking a little too grim, help comes from good old Earth!

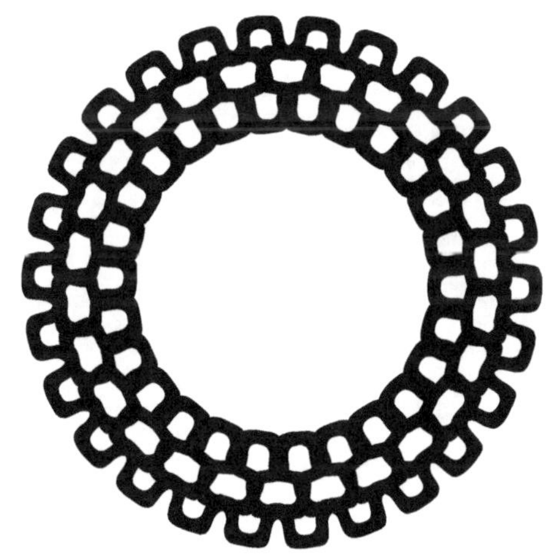

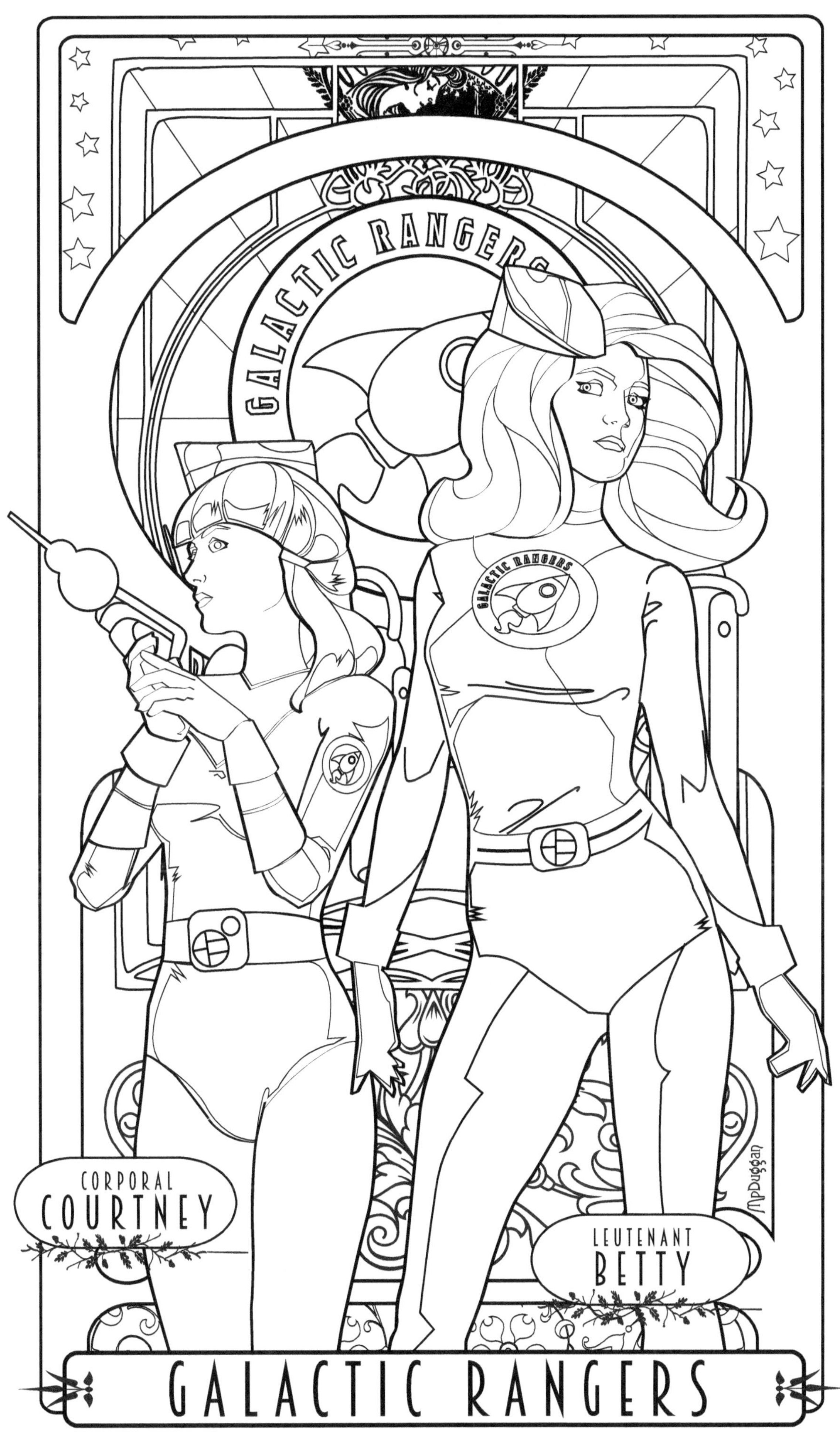
GALACTIC RANGERS
GALACTIC RANGERS
CORPORAL
COURTNEY
LEUTENANT
BETTY
GALACTIC RANGERS

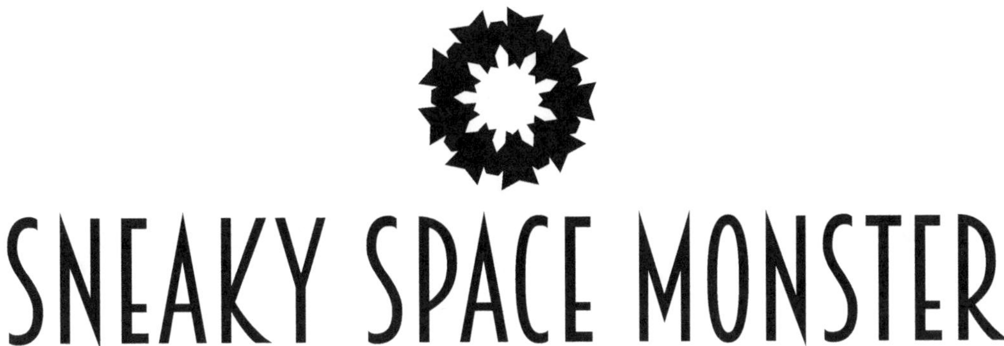

SNEAKY SPACE MONSTER

ONE OF MANY EVIL MINIONS

One of the Evil Galactic Emperor's favorite tricks is having Moon Princesses kidnapped...!

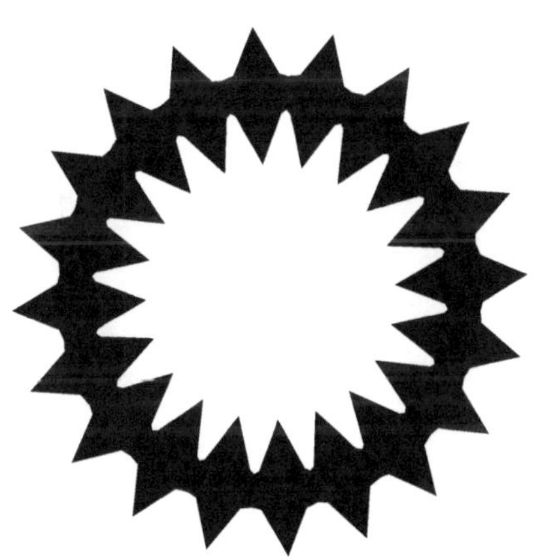

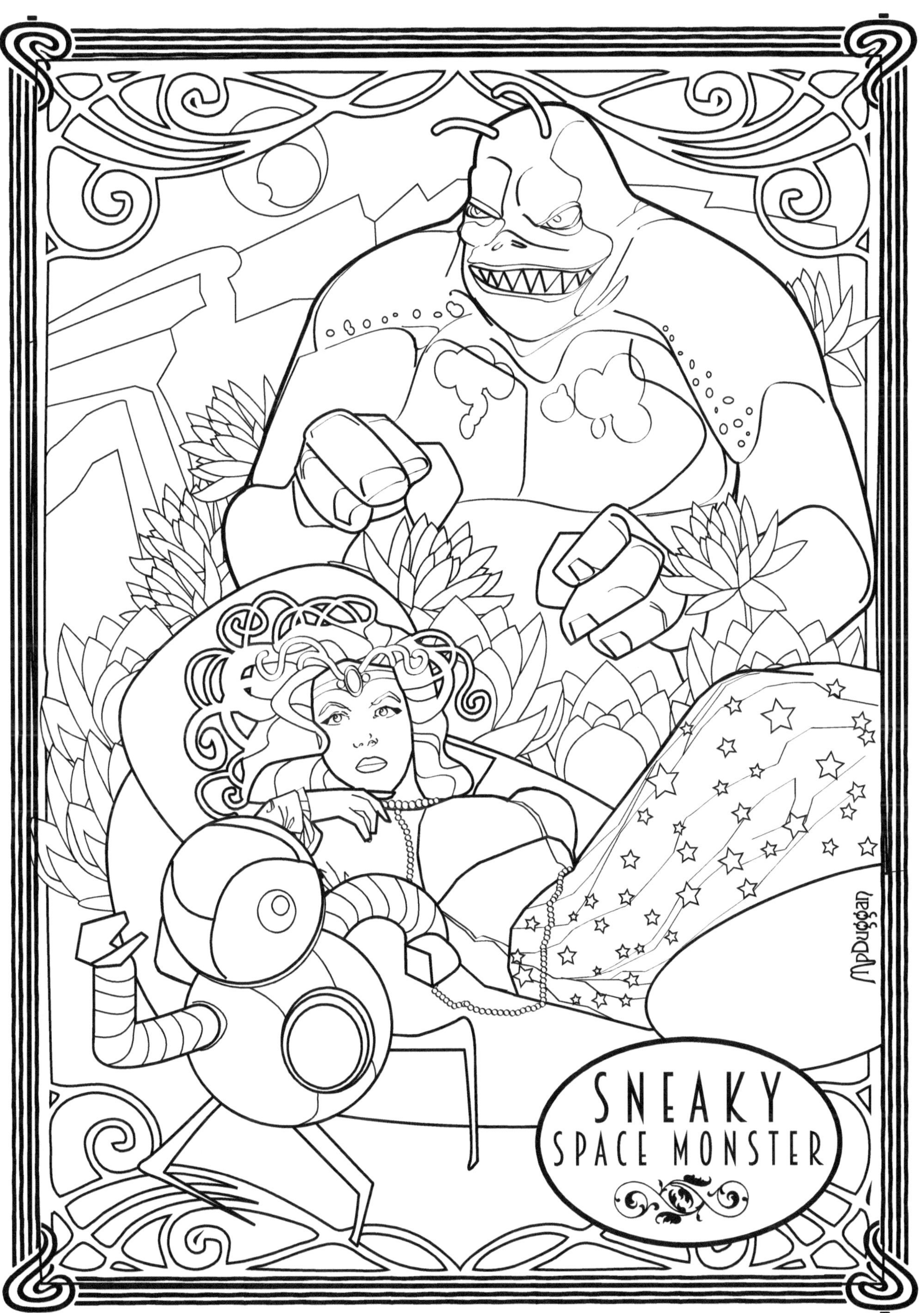
SNEAKY
SPACE MONSTER
MpDuggan

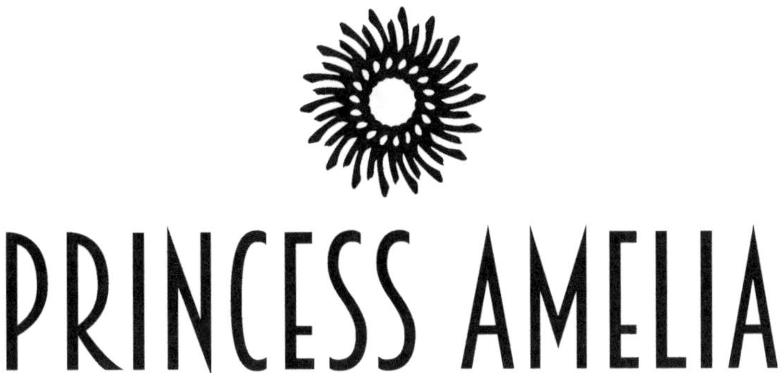

PRINCESS AMELIA

RULER OF CHARON, AND NOT A GOOD FRIEND

When push comes to shove, some people don't realize when they're getting drawn in to evil. Sadly, this is the case with Princess Amelia, who will have some explaining to do when it's all over.

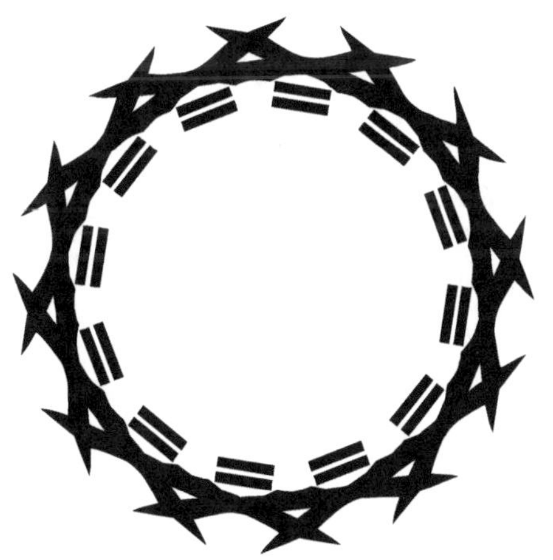

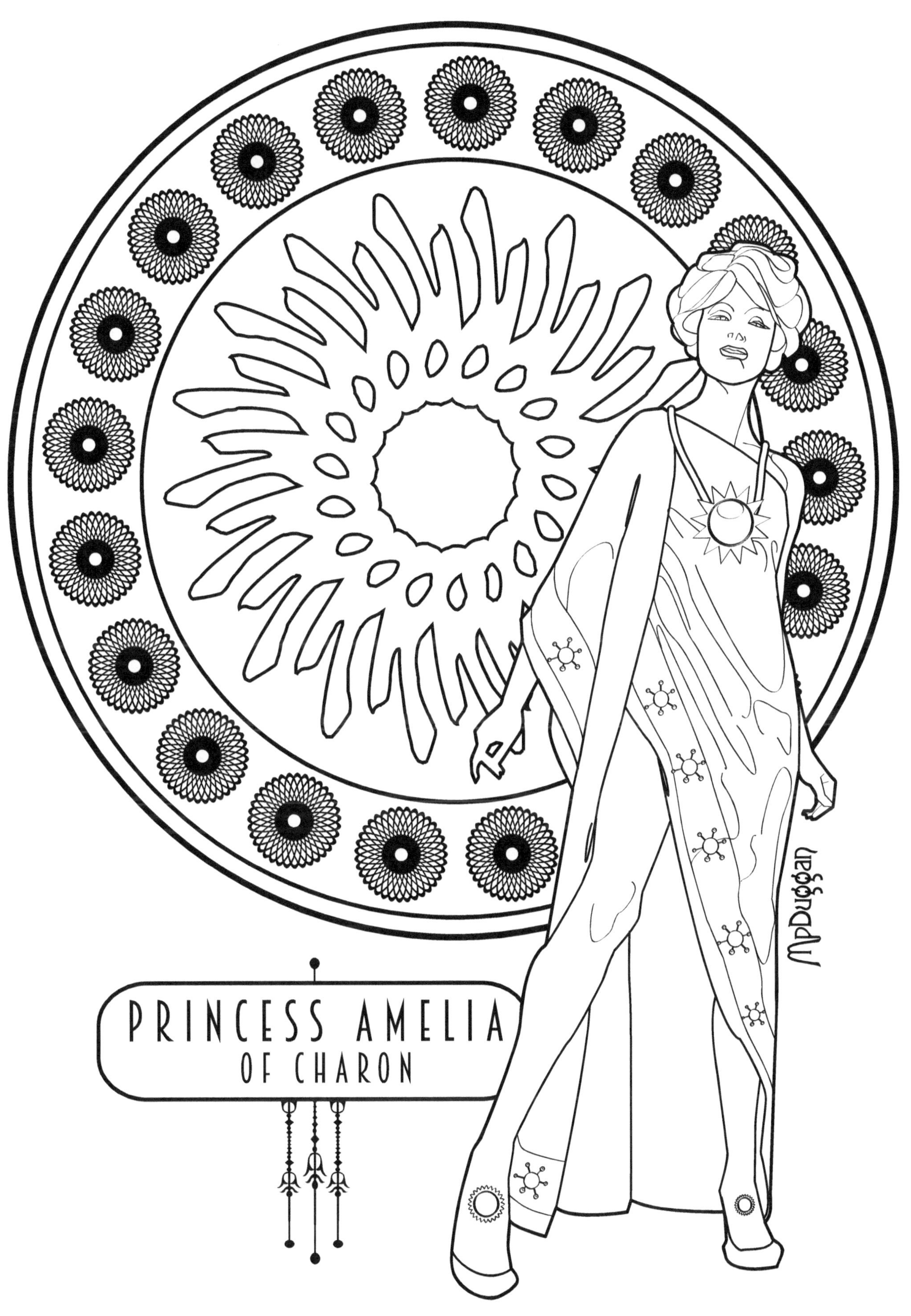
PRINCESS AMELIA
OF CHARON

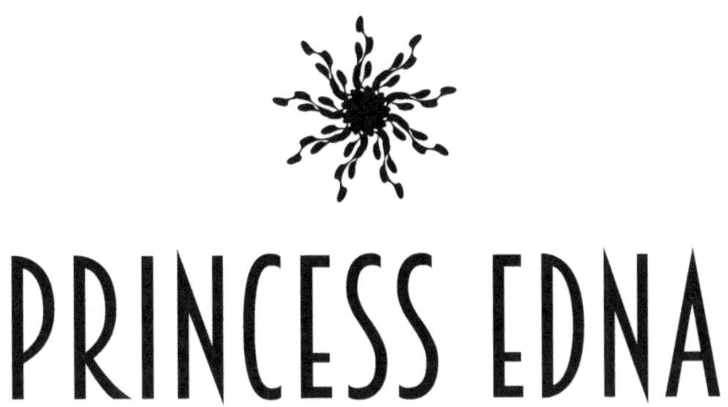

PRINCESS EDNA

A TEMPTING PROBLEM

She doesn't mean to be bad. It just sort of happens.

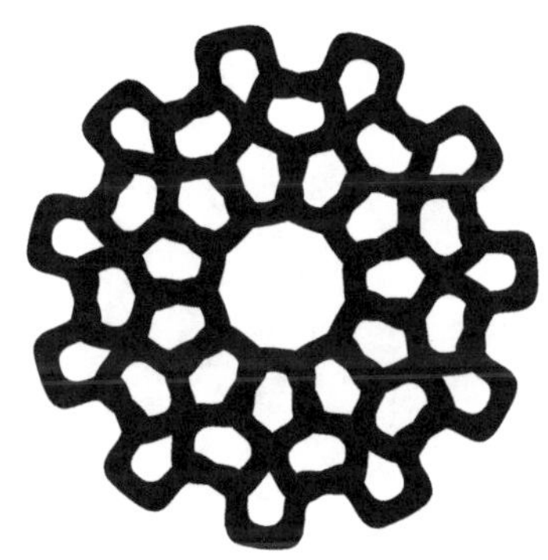

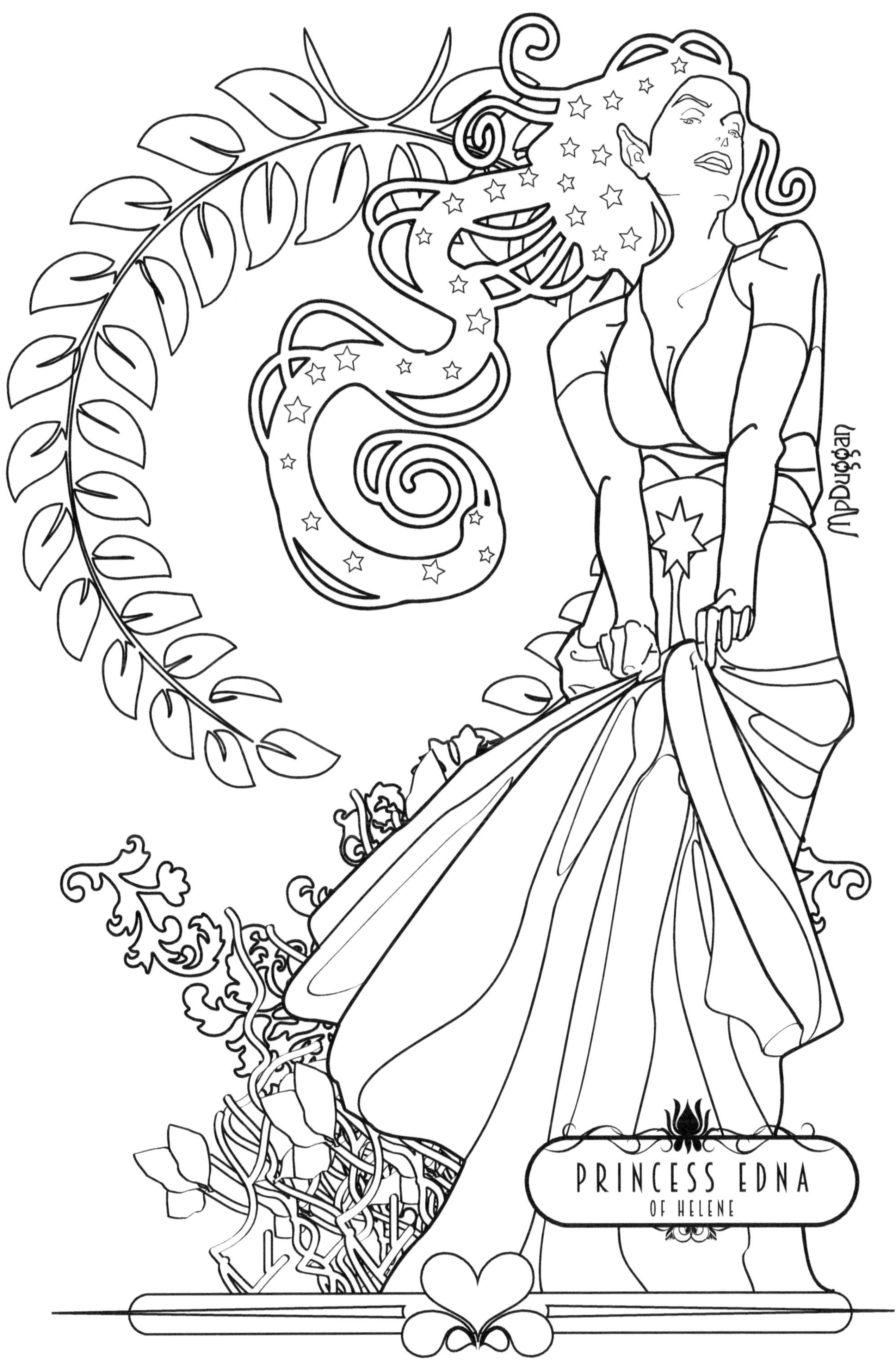
MpDuggan
PRINCESS EDNA
OF HELENE

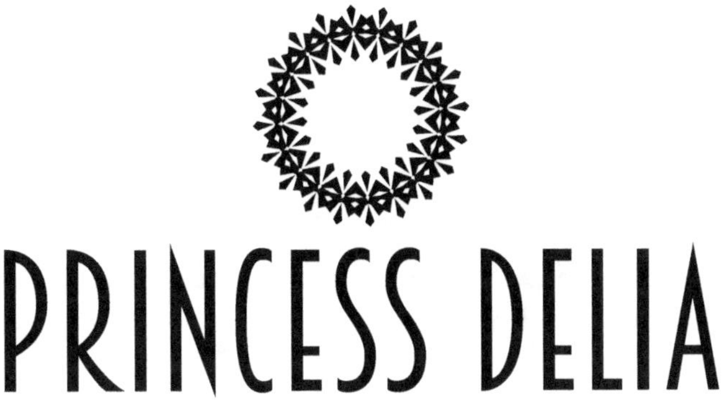

PRINCESS DELIA

A COLD MIND

Wise enough to know better, but prefers to wait and see who wins.

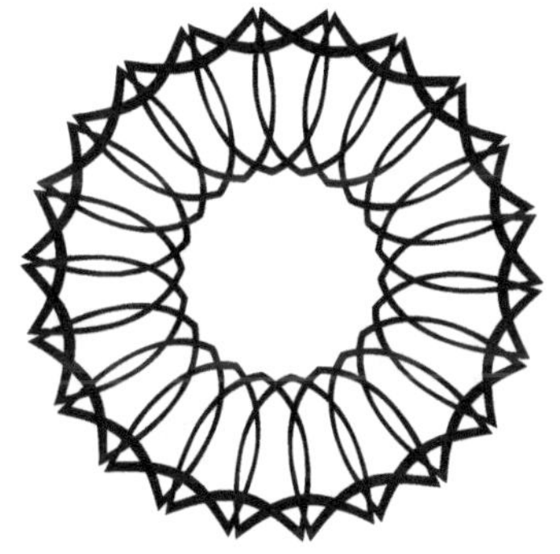

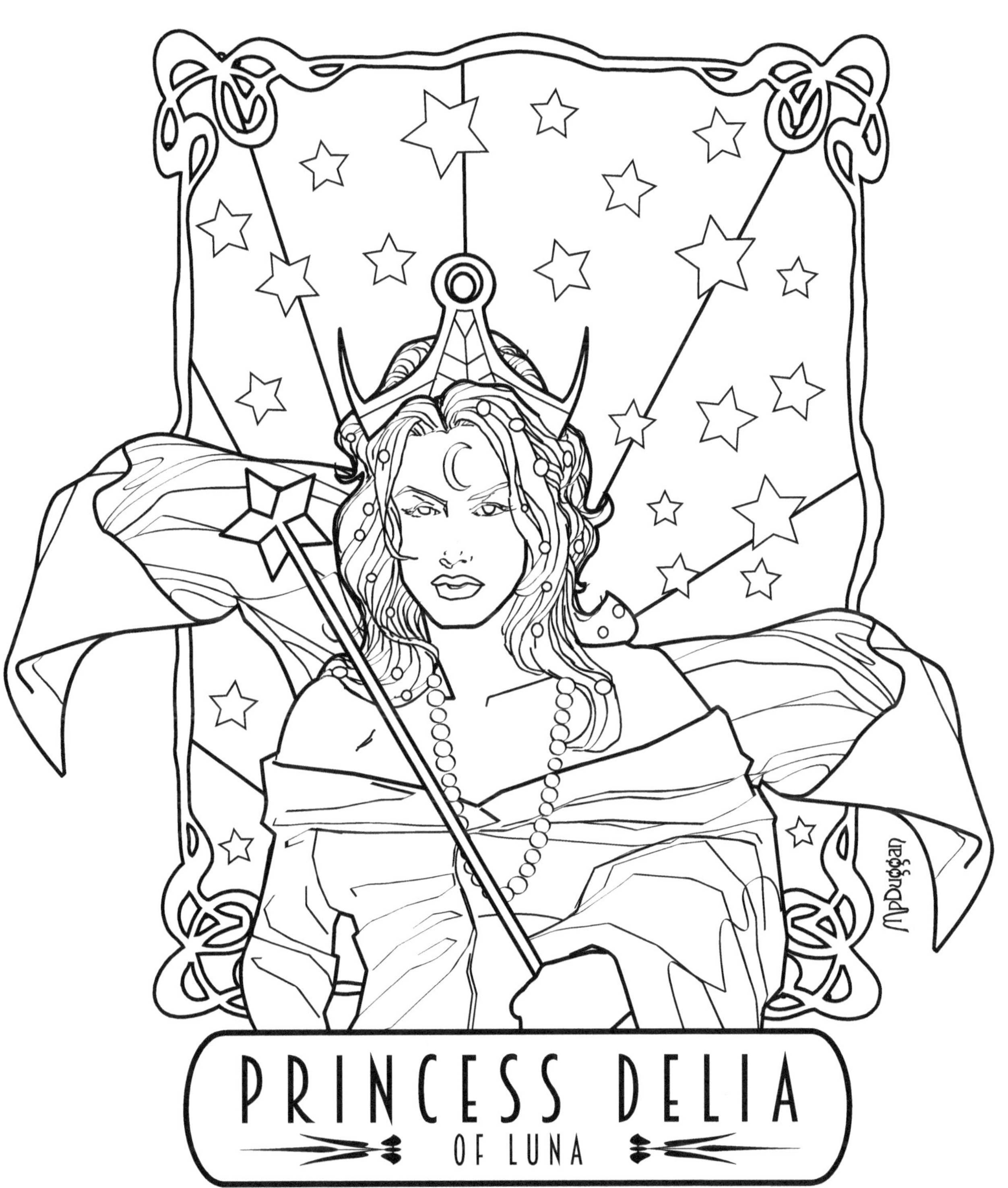
PRINCESS DELIA
OF LUNA

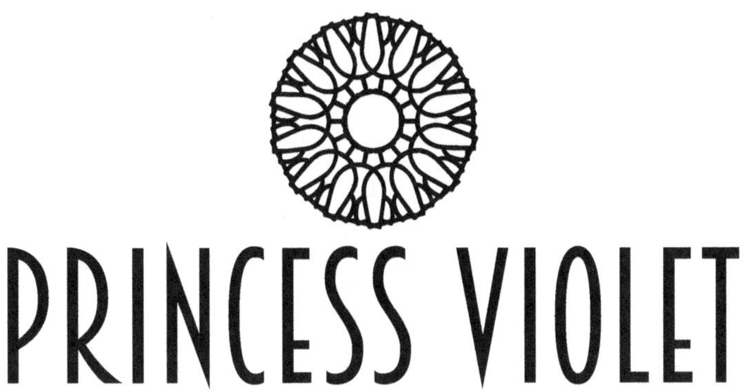

PRINCESS VIOLET

AND THE GIANT SPORES

At first too busy with her scientific discoveries, Princess Violet finally joins the forces of good just when everyone thought they were about to lose the fight.

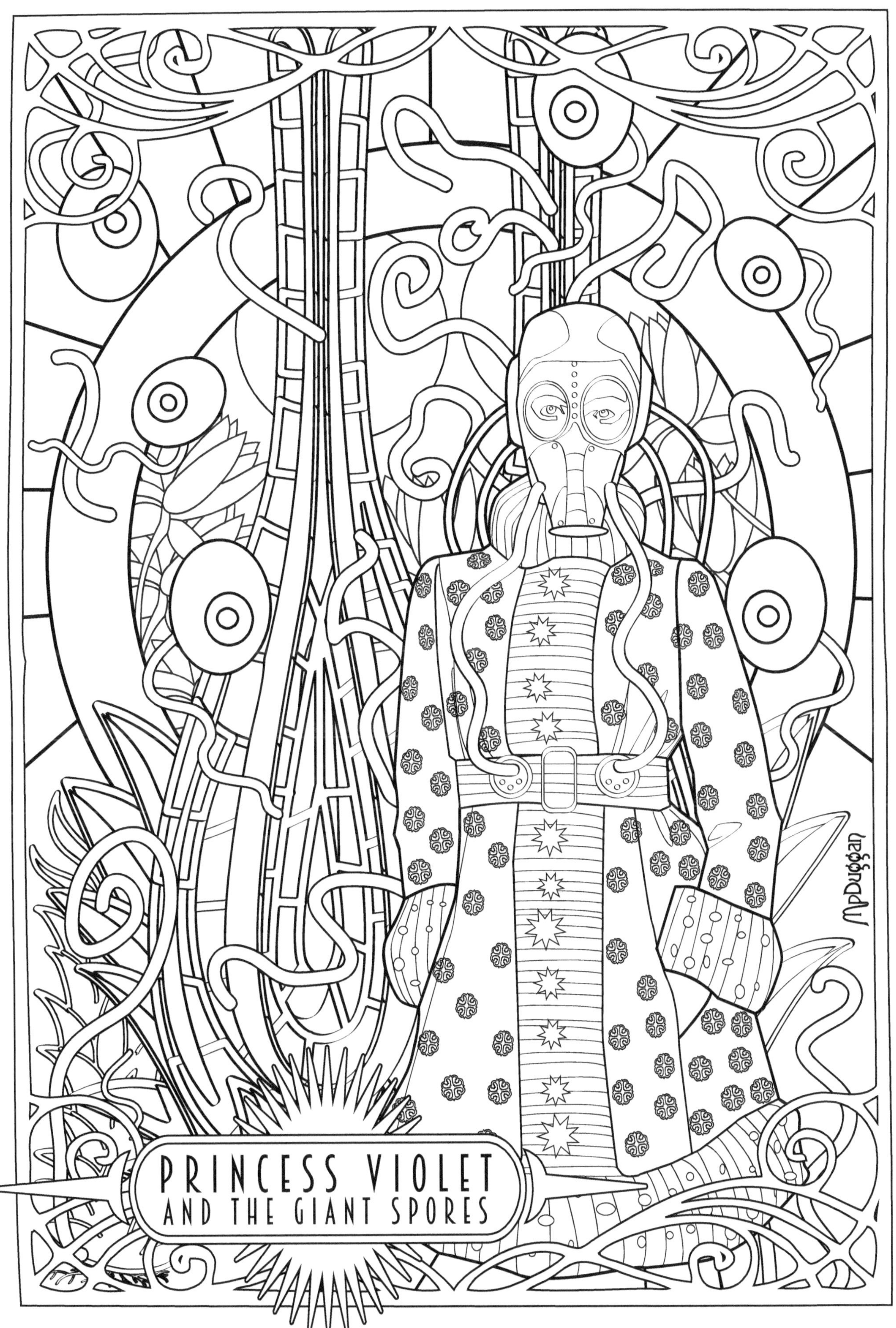
PRINCESS VIOLET
AND THE GIANT SPORES
MpDuggan

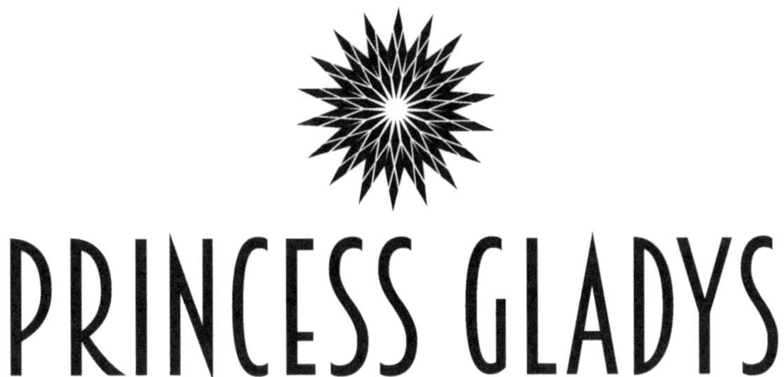

PRINCESS GLADYS

CARE-FREE BUT READY TO FIGHT

While she would prefer to be doing something else, this princess knows that evil cannot be tolerated.

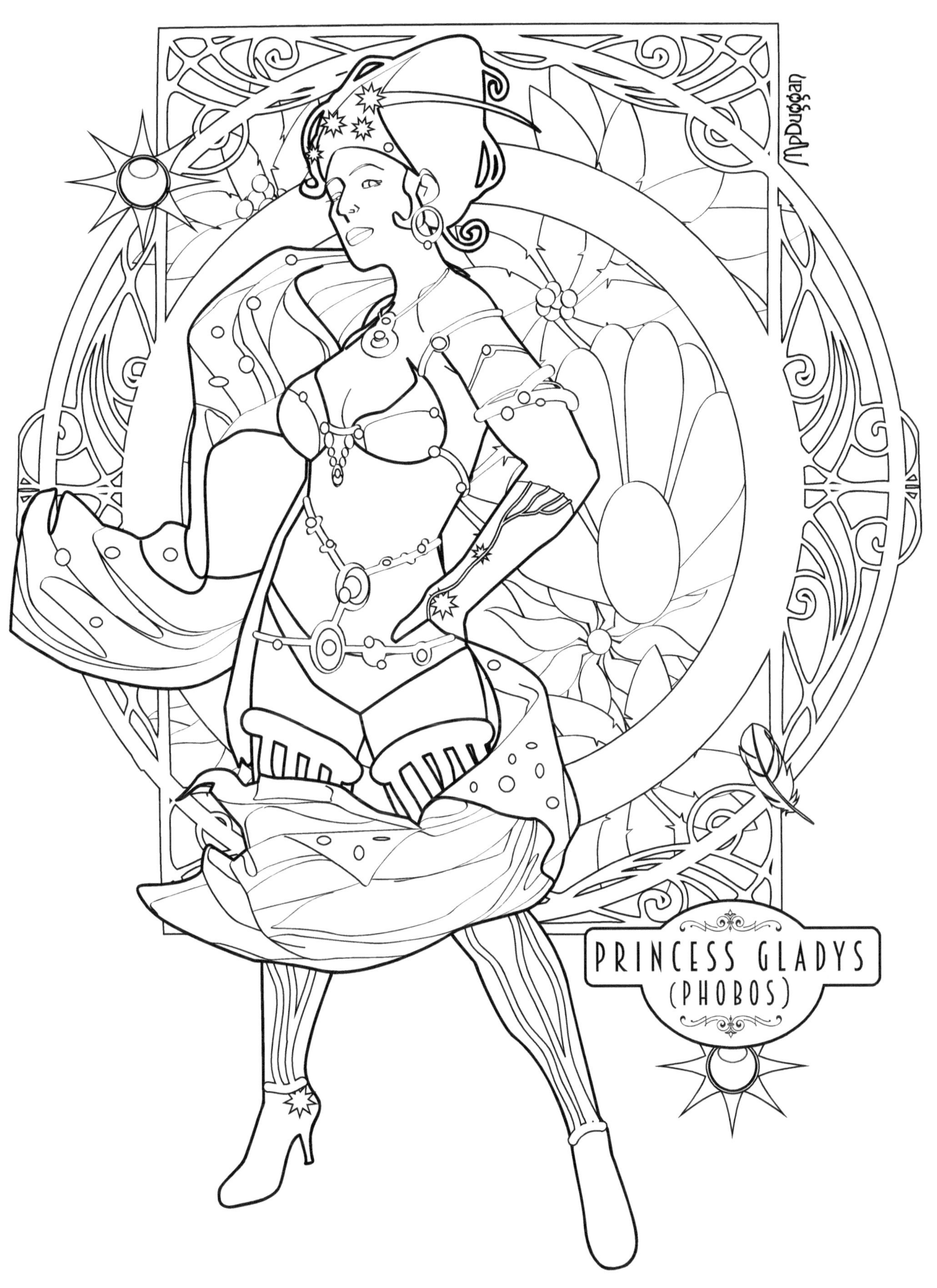
PRINCESS GLADYS
(PHOBOS)

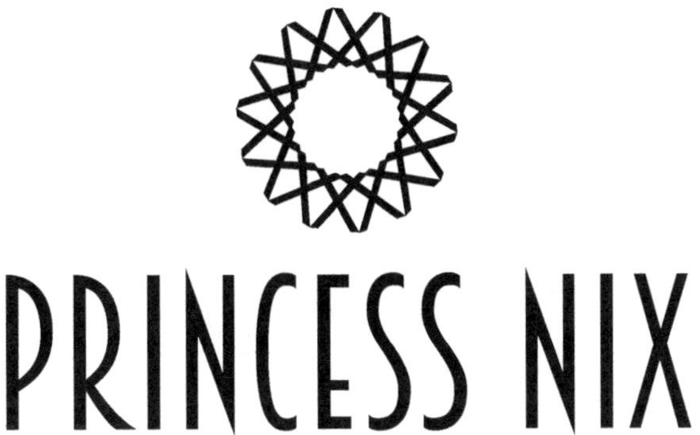

PRINCESS NIX

EVIL DAUGHTER #1

When she isn't trying to murder her sister, Princess Nix is sending out her minions to further her father's evil mission.

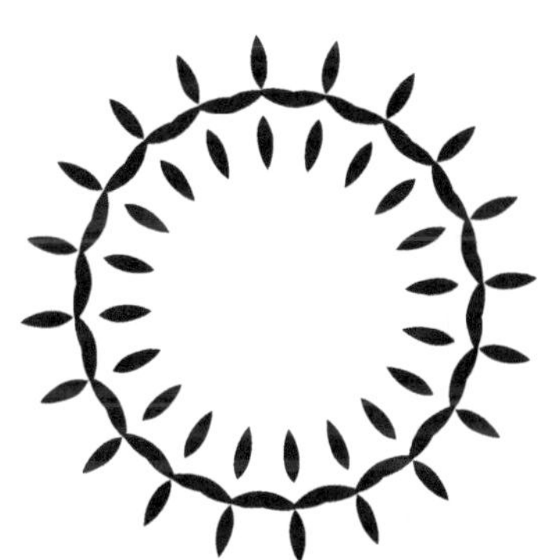

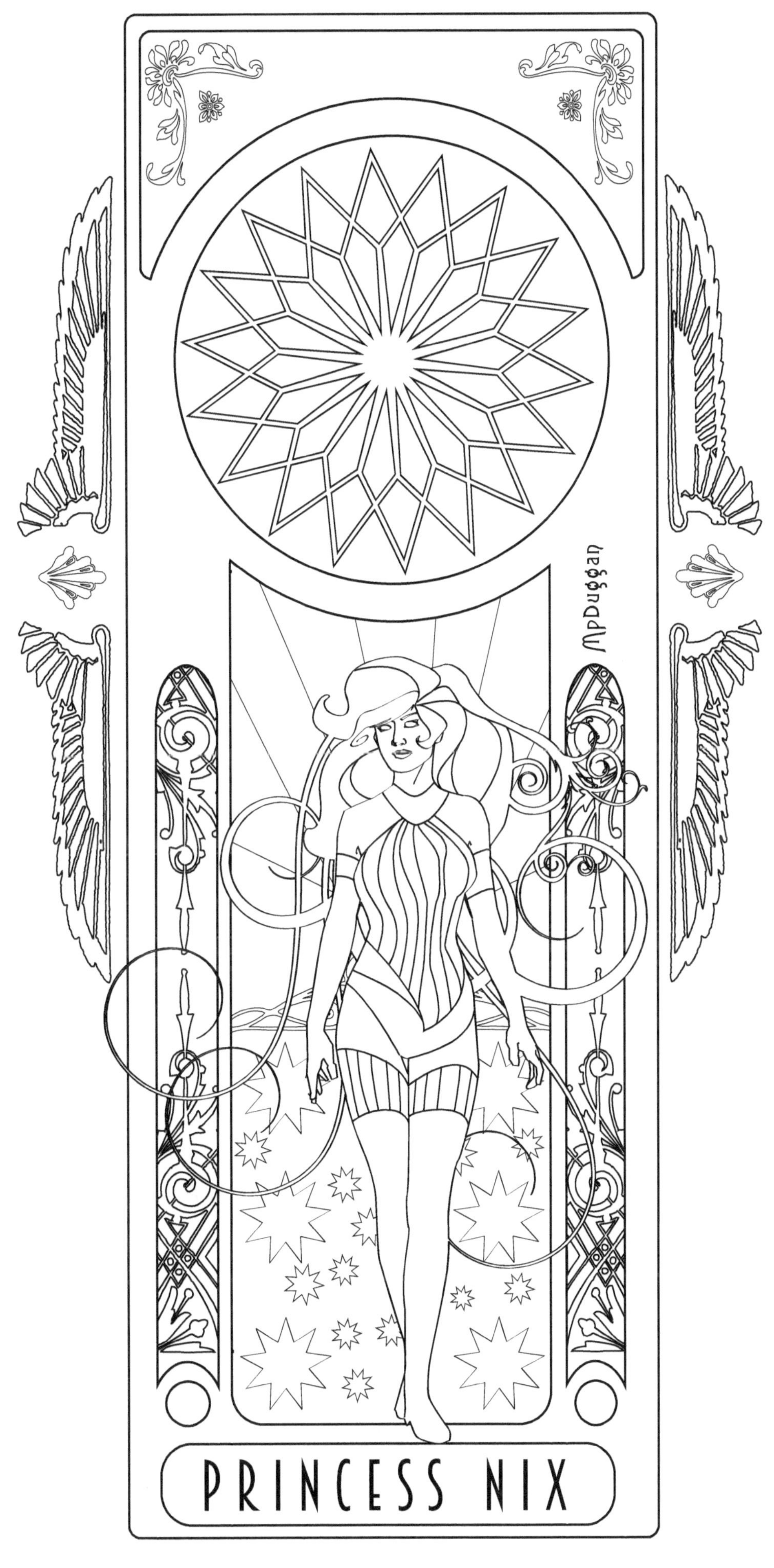
McDuggan
PRINCESS NIX

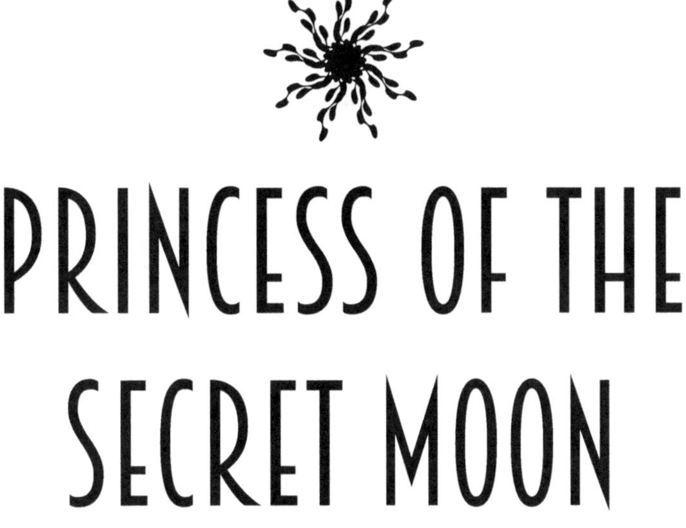

PRINCESS OF THE SECRET MOON

A QUIET ALLY

Secretly coordinating with her cousion, Princess Veronica, and keeping tabs on the evil daughters.

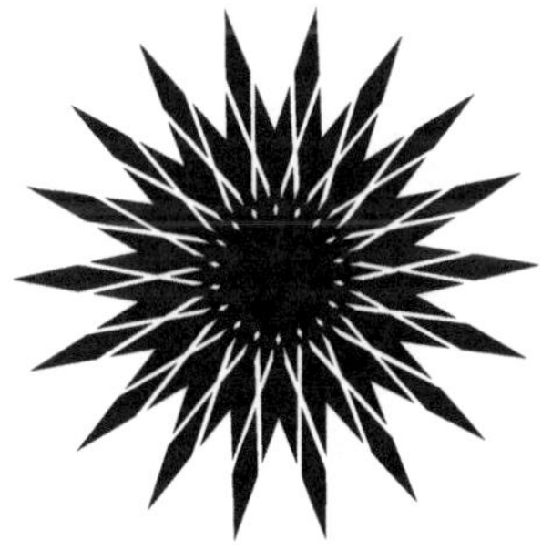

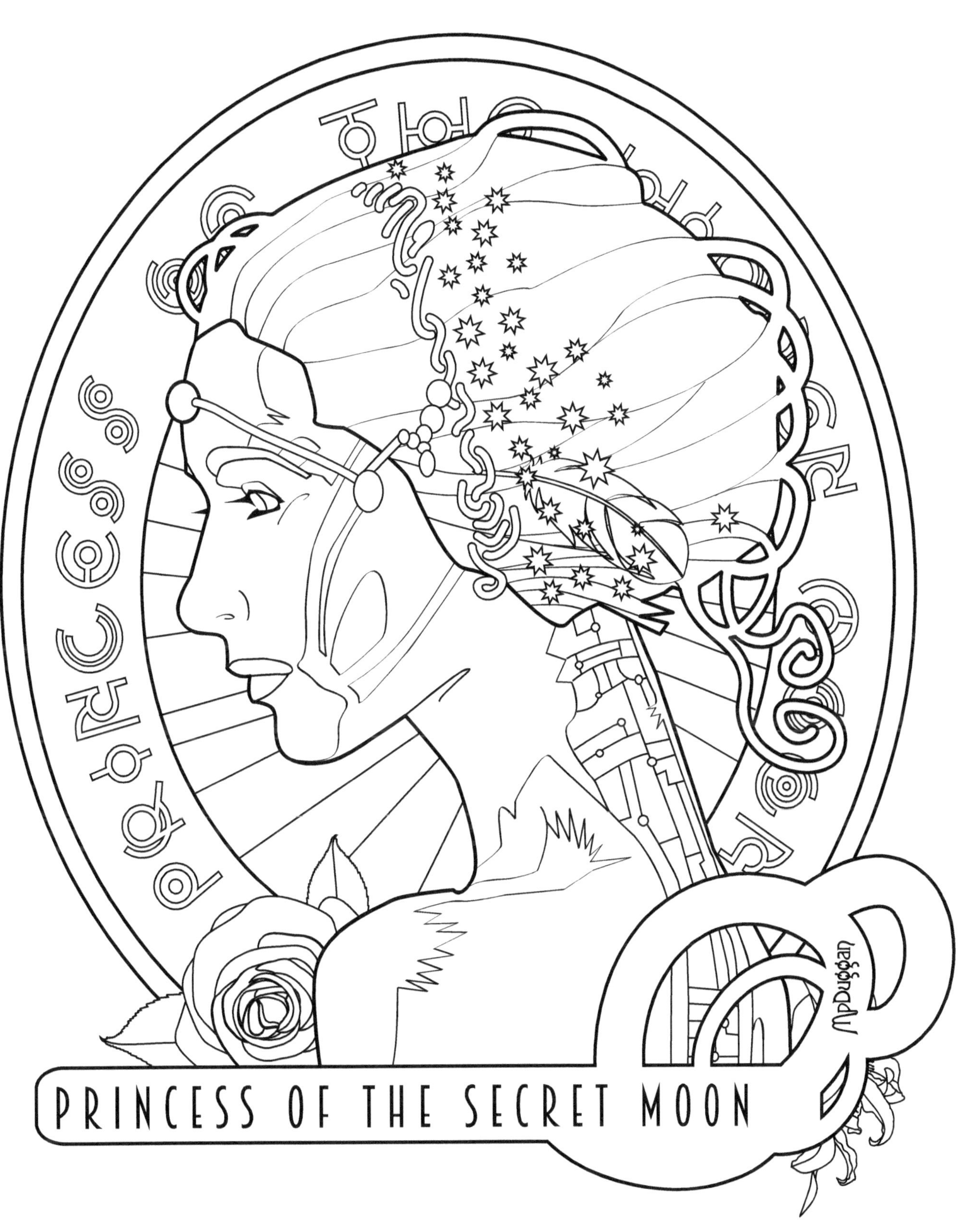
PRINCESS OF THE SECRET MOON

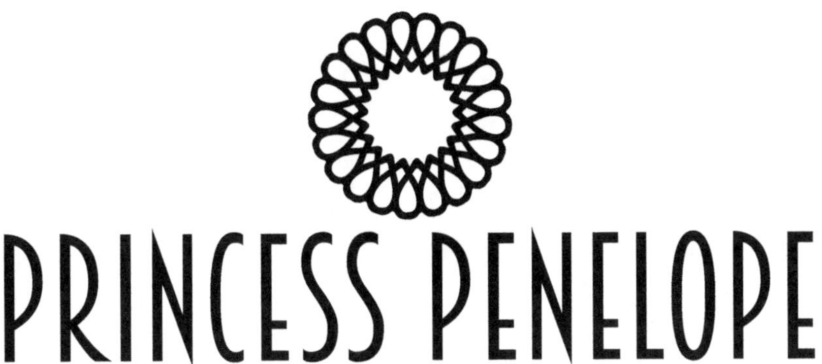

PRINCESS PENELOPE

NEUTRAL MEANS NO

Really, who has time for galactic wars, these days?

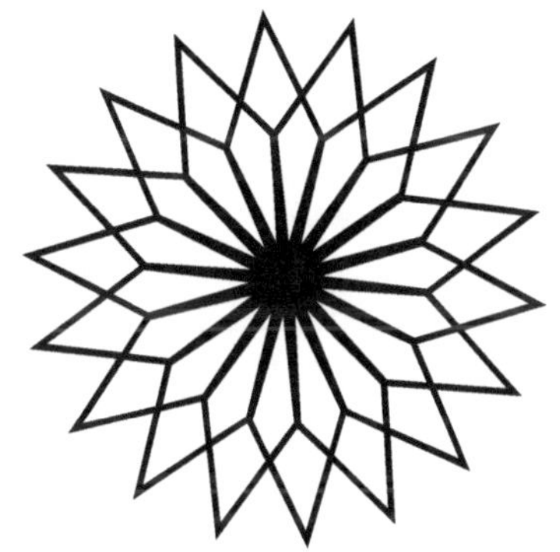

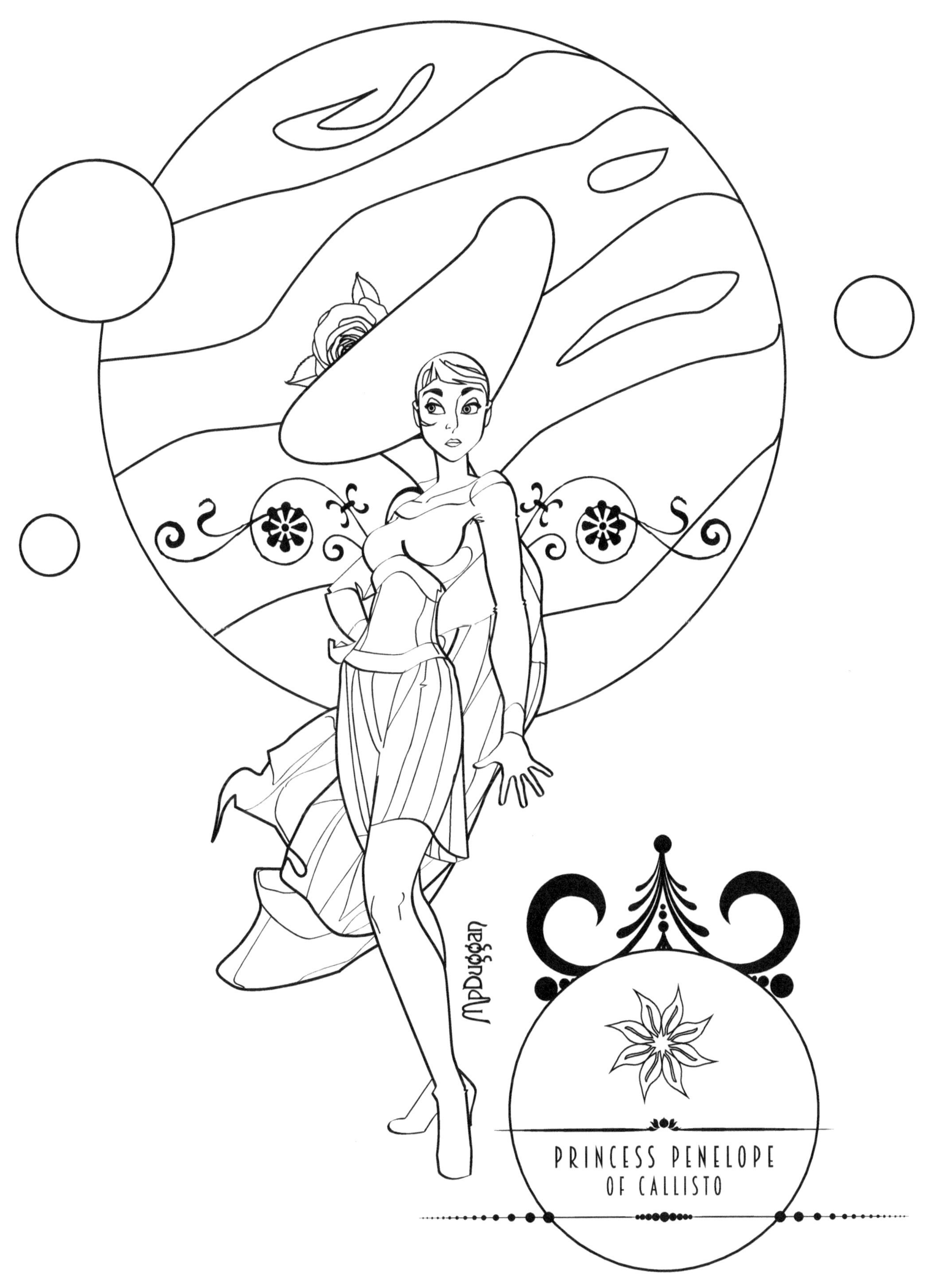
MpDuggan 33
PRINCESS PENELOPE
OF CALLISTO

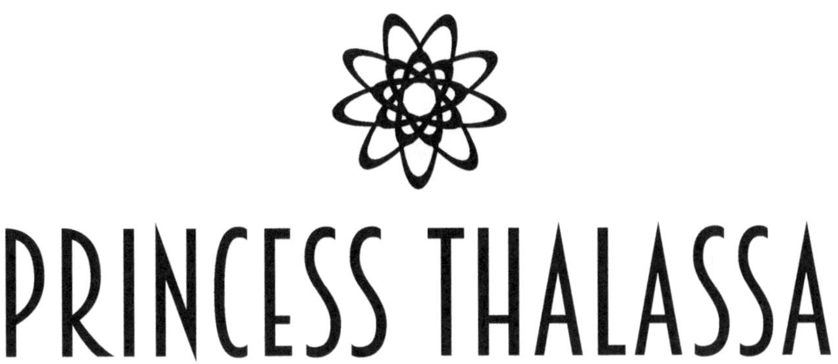

PRINCESS THALASSA

EVIL DAUGHTER #2

From the depths of her under-water moon, this evil daughter contrives to further her father's evil agenda--all the while avoiding the assassin's knife.

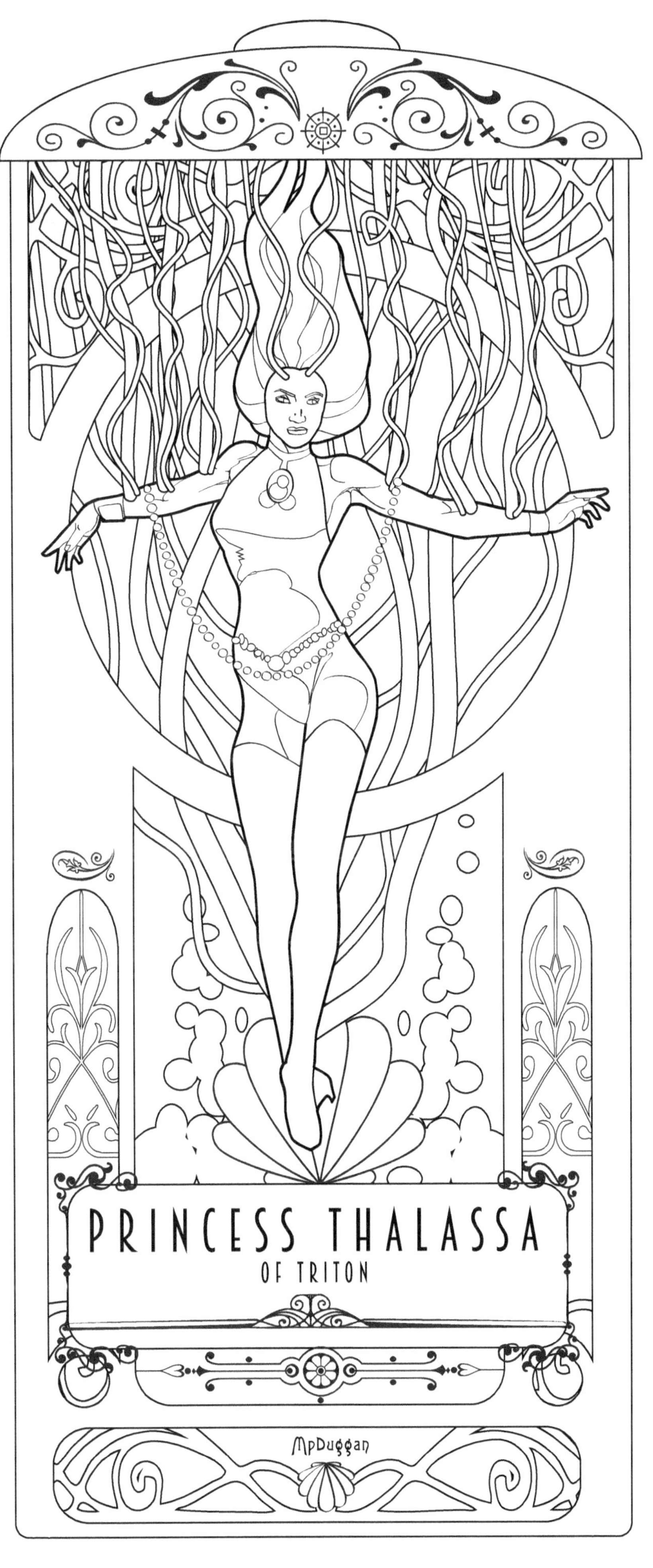
PRINCESS THALASSA
OF TRITON
MpDuggan

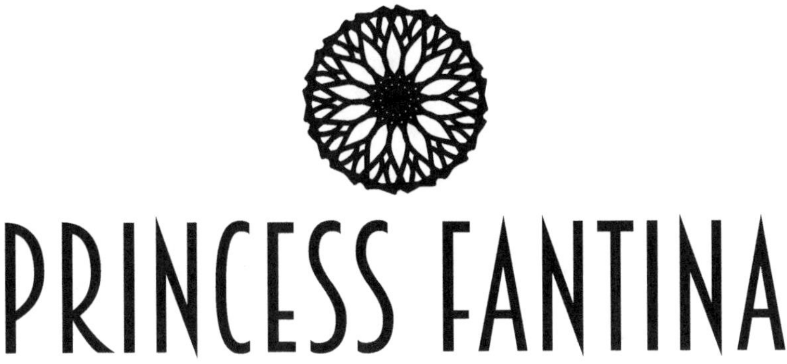

PRINCESS FANTINA

LOST HER PATIENCE, AND ALMOST HER KINGDOM ALONG WITH IT

Beautiful, but unwise--when she heard about all the evil things the Emperor was doing, she sent a letter of complaint. Right after that the dark soldiers arrived, and she's been holed up in her citadel ever since.

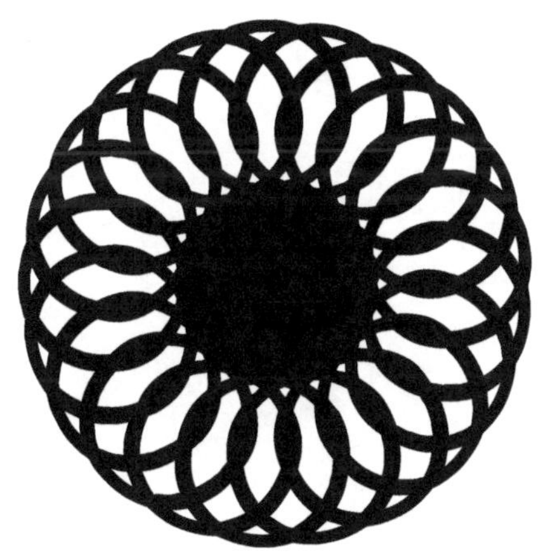

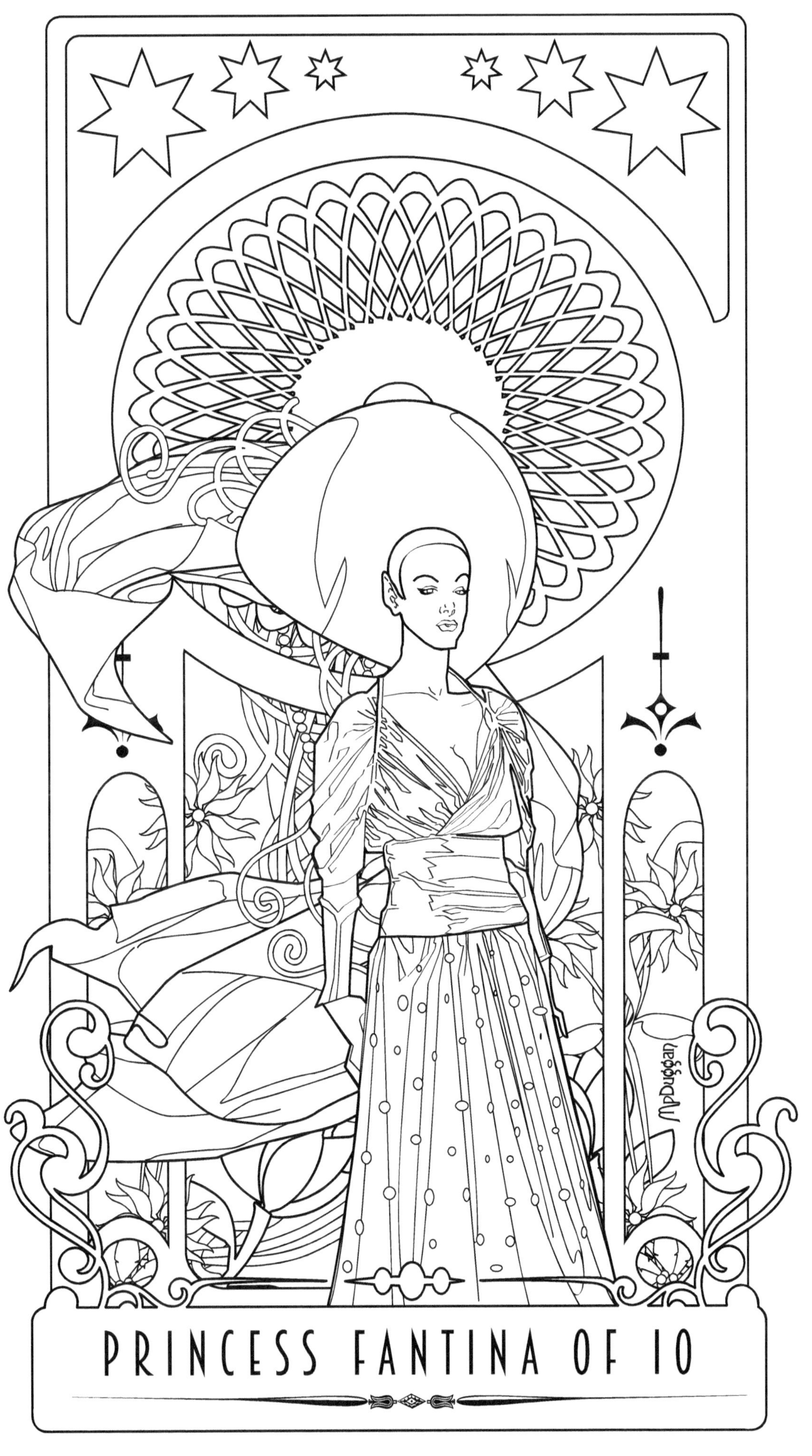
PRINCESS FANTINA OF IO

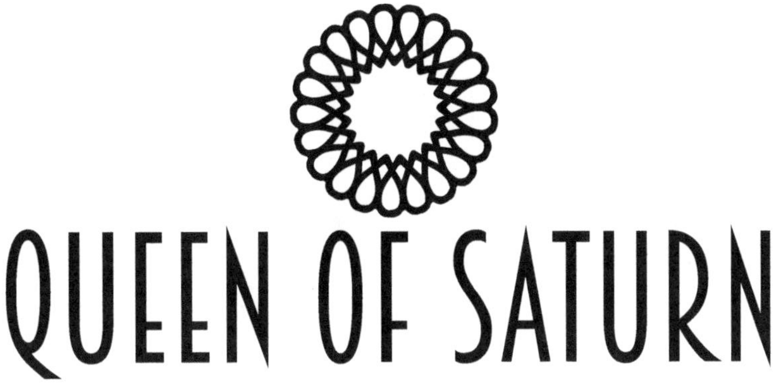

QUEEN OF SATURN

TRIED TO STAY NEUTRAL, BUT THAT DIDN'T WORK

Famous for her space yacht parties, the Queen of Saturn was content to stay out of it--until the Evil Emperor sent his soldiers to kidnap her. After a nasty fight, she's ready to step up.

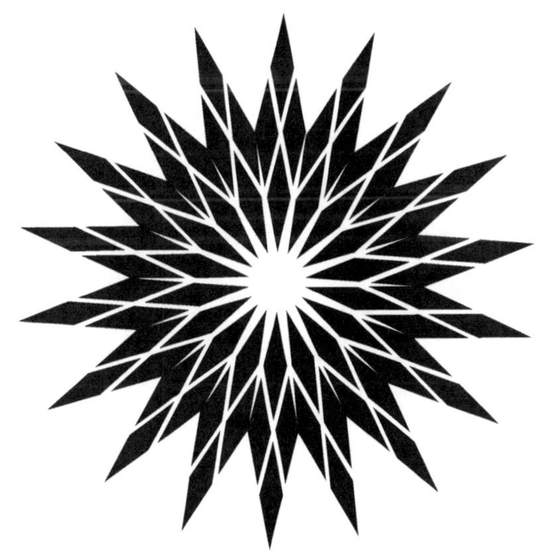

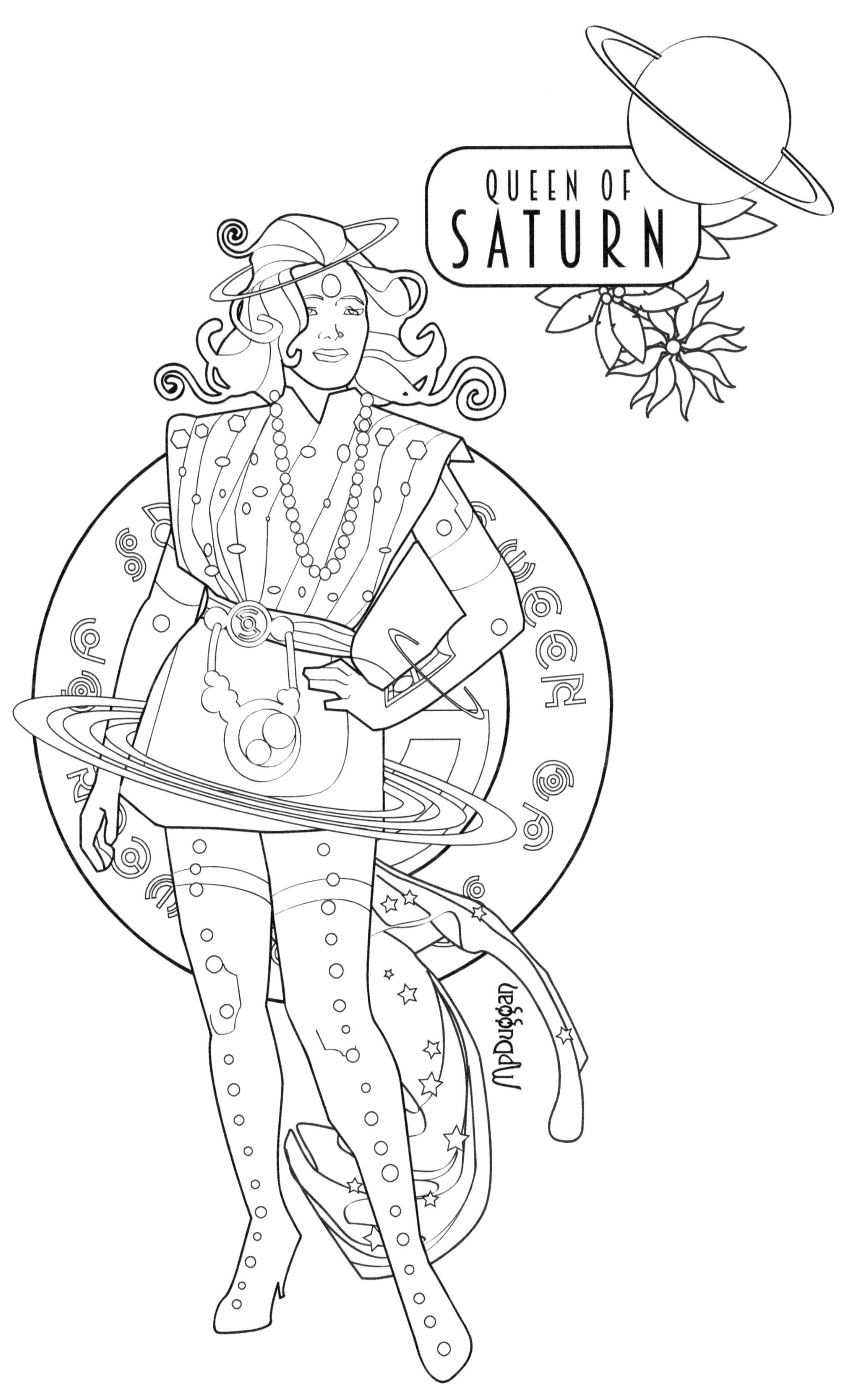
QUEEN OF
SATURN
MpDuggan

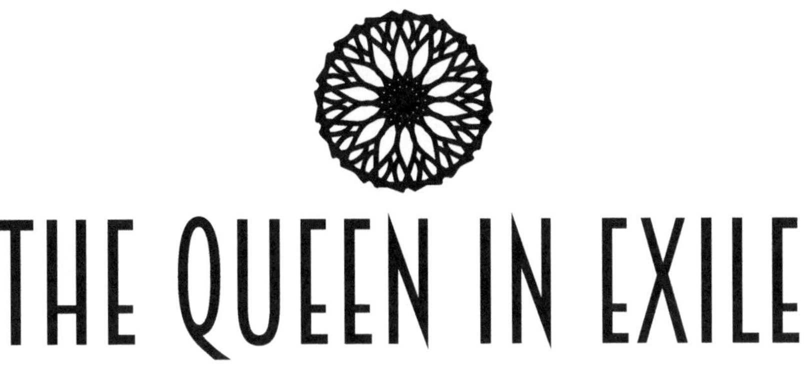

THE QUEEN IN EXILE

BANISHED, BUT NOT FORGOTTEN

No one knows where the Emperor’s wife went.

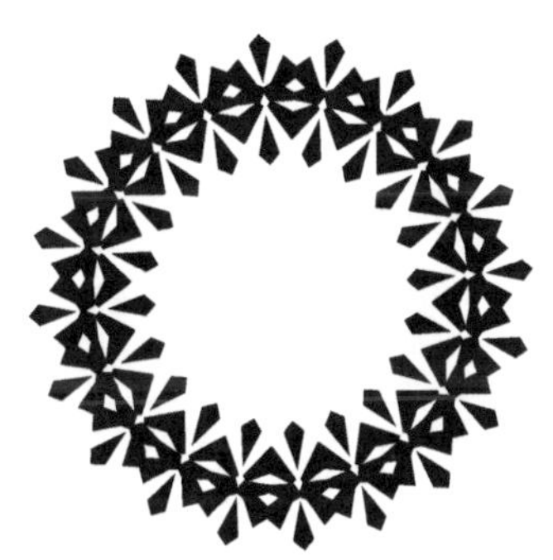

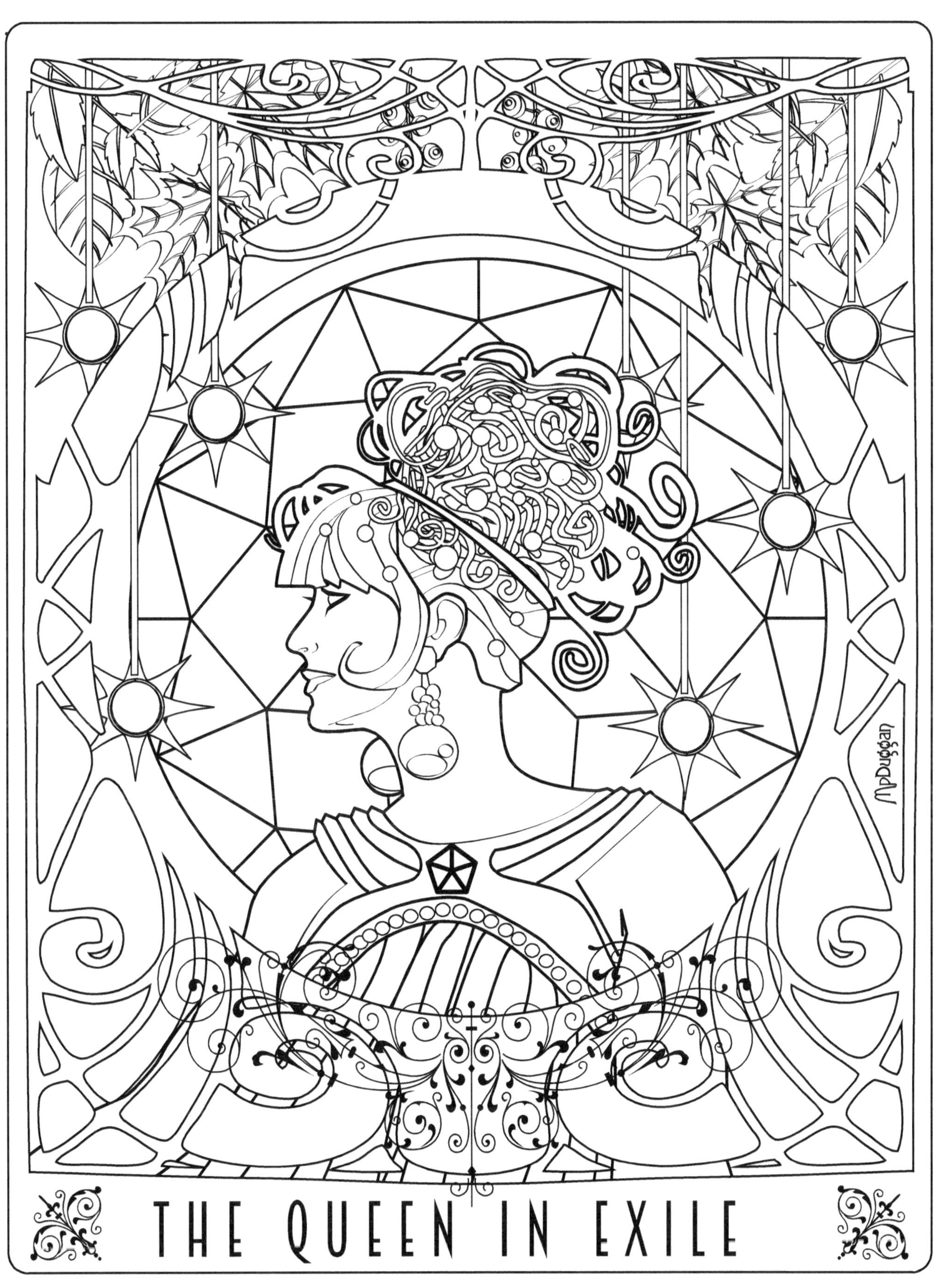
THE QUEEN IN EXILE

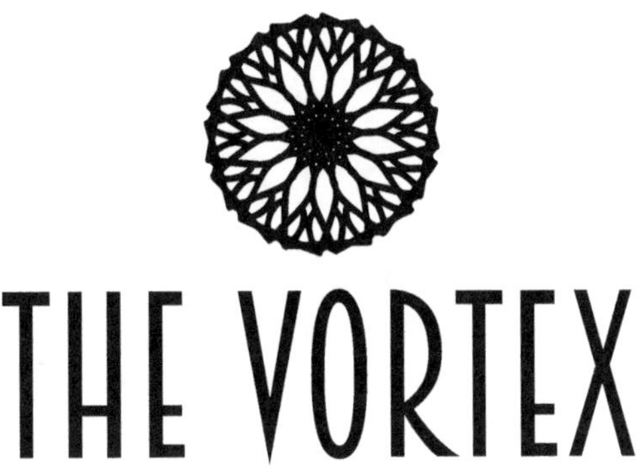

THE VORTEX

A POWERFUL FORCE

Coveted by many, this incredible portal to the other side of the galaxy is highly sought-after. But you never know where it will appear next.

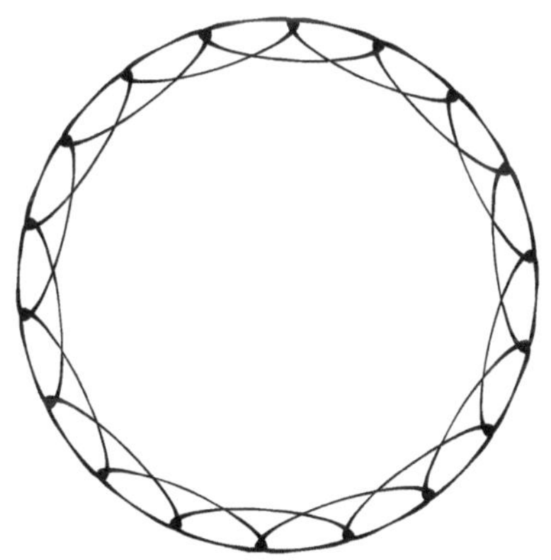

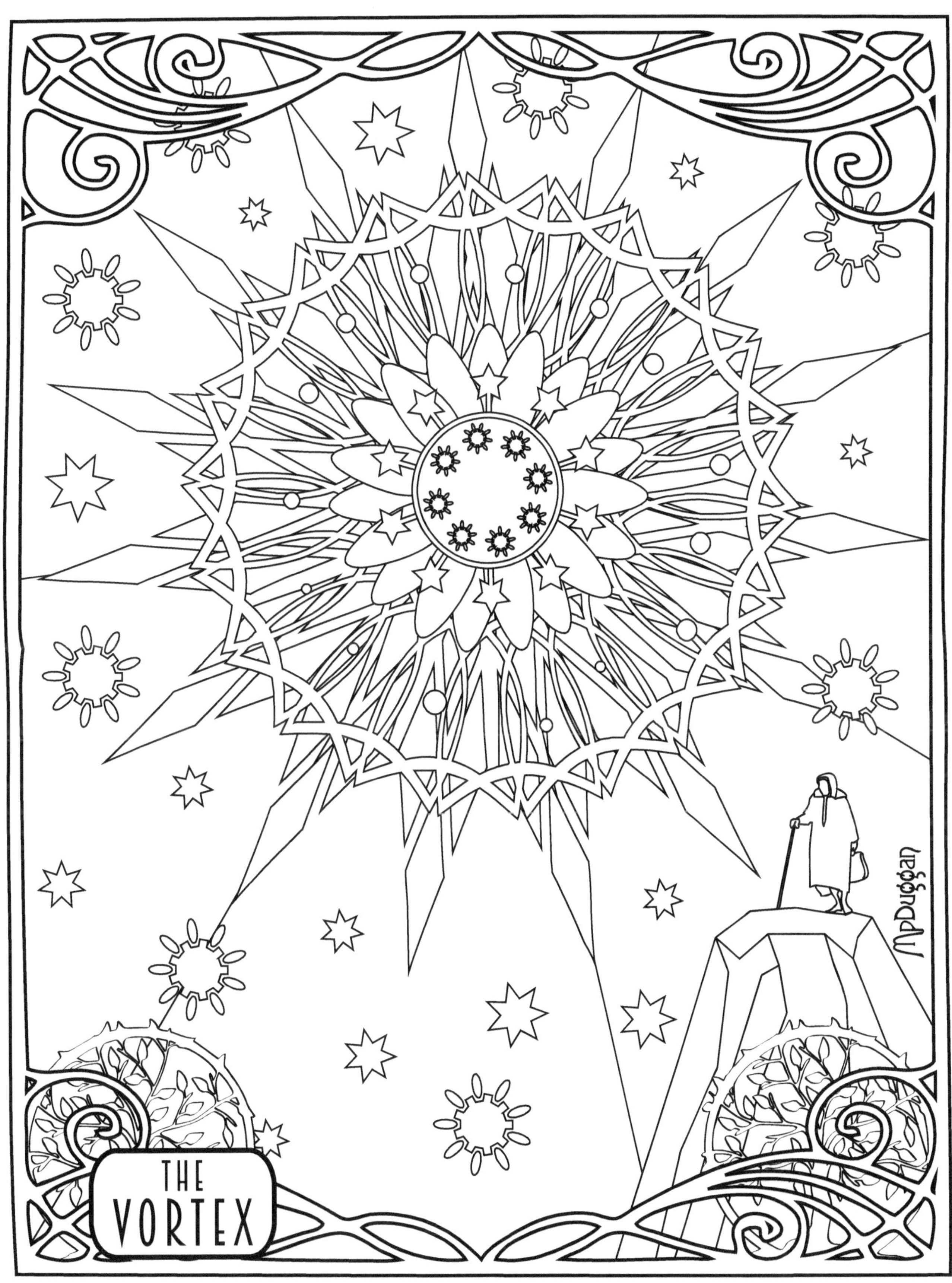
THE
VORTEX

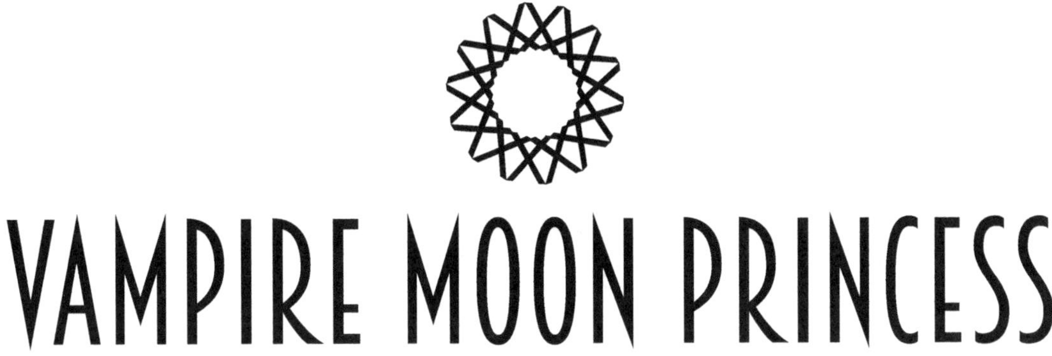

VAMPIRE MOON PRINCESS

DO NOT ACCEPT THE BRUNCH INVITE

She's an equal opportunity offender, and always thirsty.

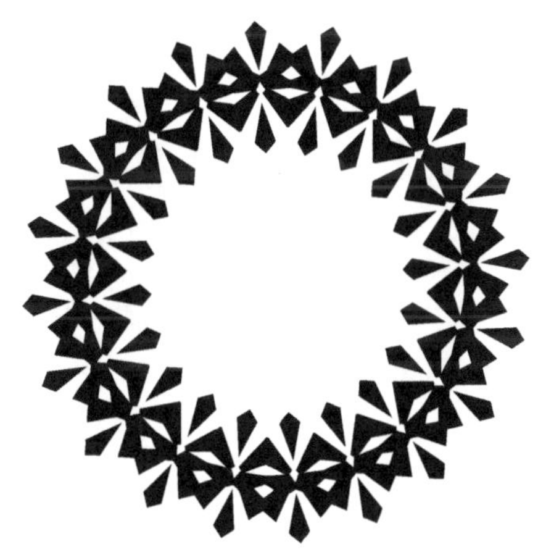

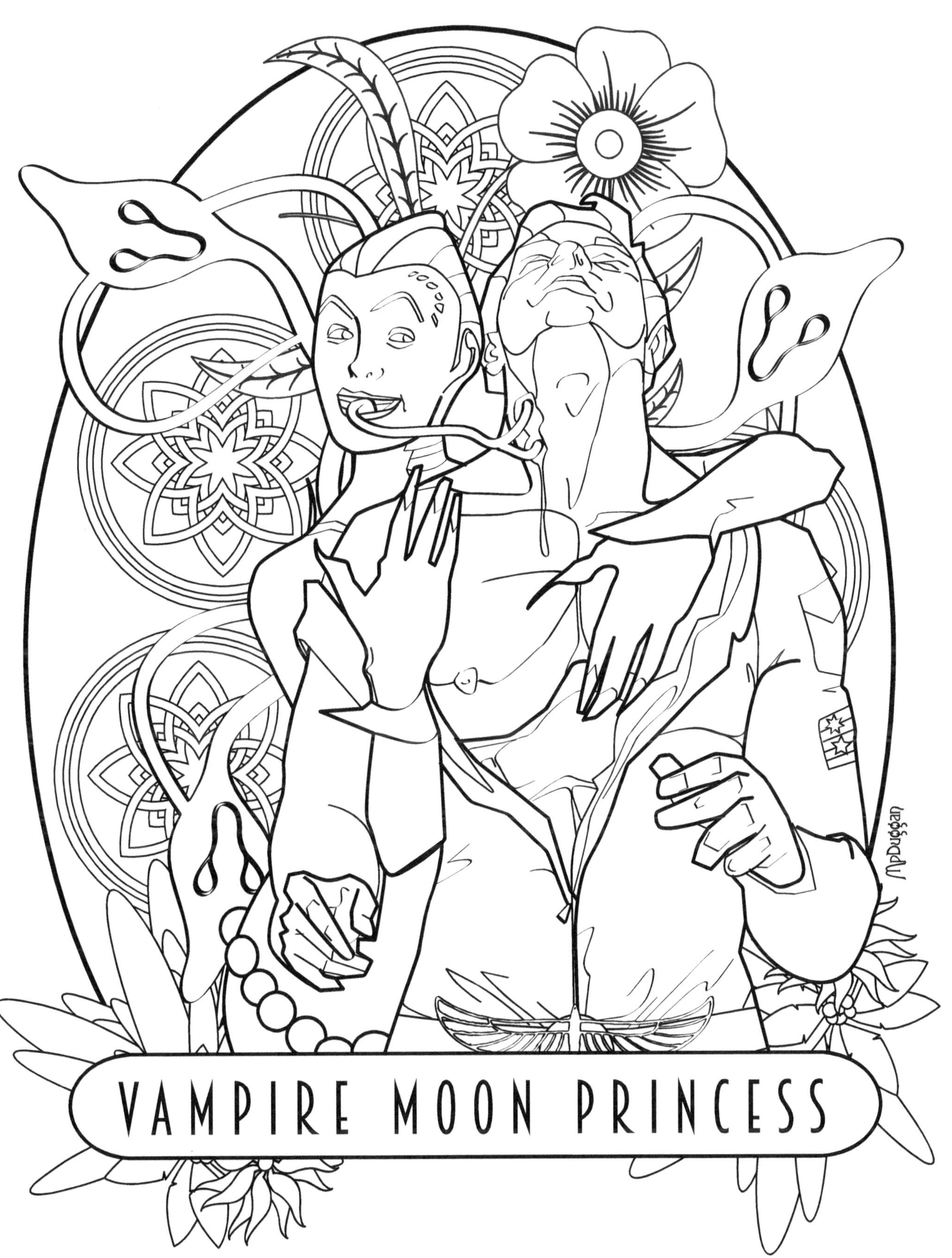
VAMPIRE MOON PRINCESS

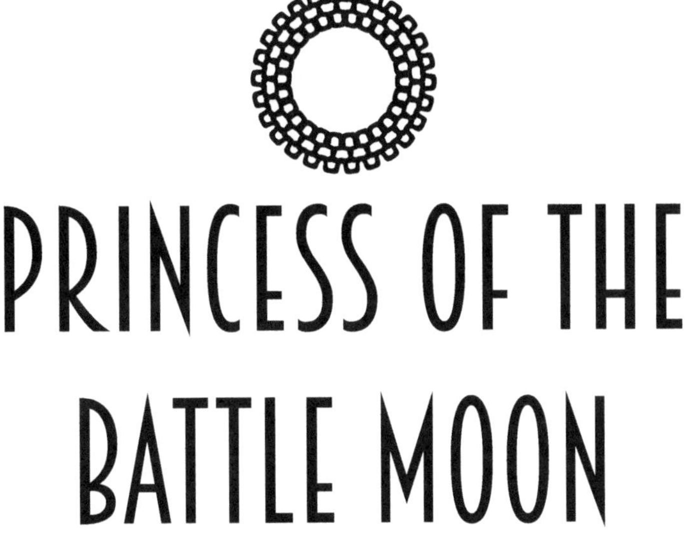

PRINCESS OF THE BATTLE MOON

SHE LOVES A GOOD FIGHT

The battle moon is where the greatest warriors are trained.

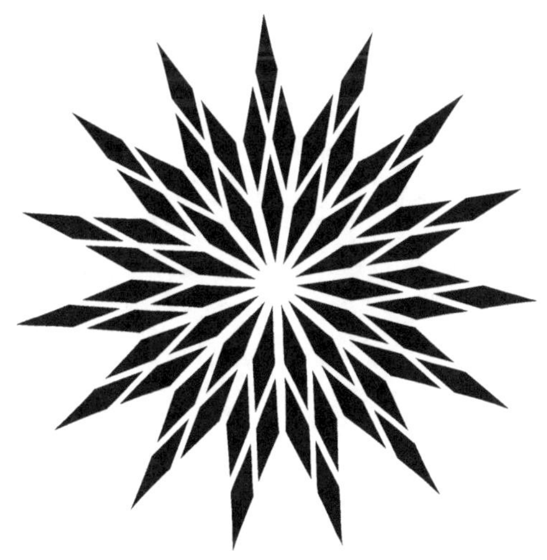

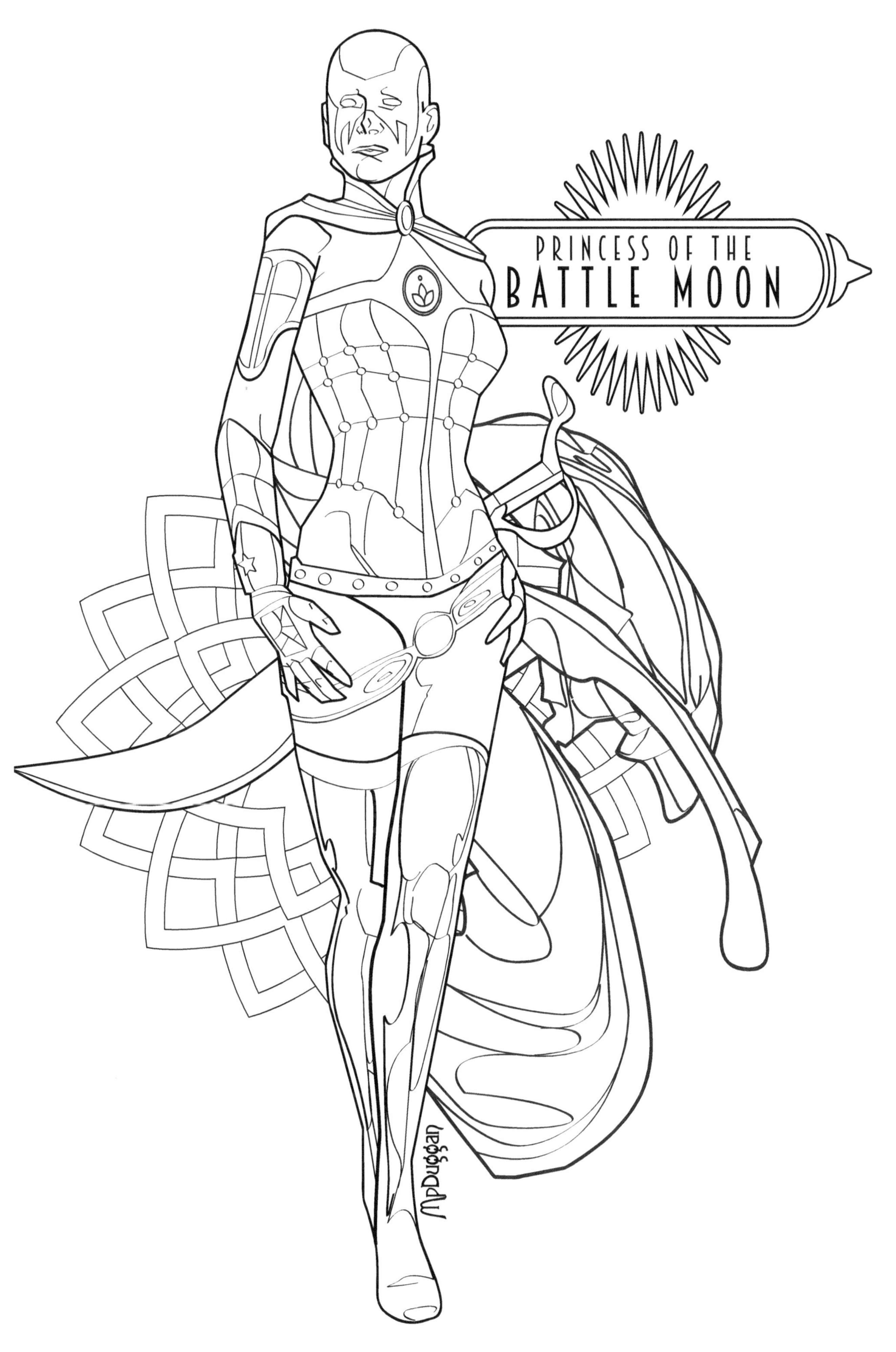
PRINCESS OF THE
BATTLE MOON
MpDuggan

MOON PRINCESSES AND SPACE MONSTERS

COLORING BOOK

WRITTEN AND ILLUSTRATED BY M. PATRICK DUGGAN

About Art Nouveau

One of my favorite art movements, it was most popular between 1890 and 1910 (a pretty short time) before being replaced by Art Deco (another favorite, frankly) and then Modernism. It was a reaction to the previous academic art of the 19th century, and was greatly inspired by nature. My work in this book is a pale shadow of the geniuses who painted, built, sculpted, and led the original movement. But I hope you enjoy it anyway. If you are interested in learning more about Art Nouveau, I recommend you seek out the works of these nouveau masters: Alphonse Mucha, Gustav Kllmt, Henri de Toulouse-Lautrec, Aubrey Beardsley, Virginia Frances Sterett, Koloman Moser, Walter Crane, Kay Nielsen, Jan Toorop, Stanislaw Wyspianski, Will H. Bradley, and Jules Cheret, just to name a few—or Google 'Art Nouveau Artists' if you're curious, and get ready to give your eyes a treat.

As a final note, if you enjoy this book, I hope you will write and let me know? Also, if there are characters you'd like to see in a future edition, I'd love to hear your thoughts. Last, if you'd like to share your coloring of any of these pictures, I'd love to see them!

Thank you, and have a wonderful day.
M. Patrick Duggan

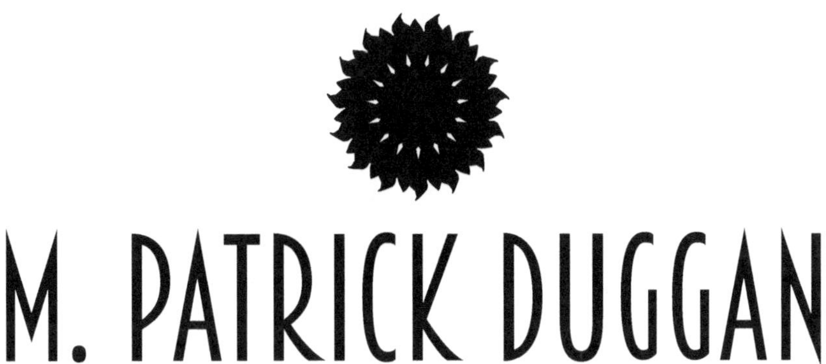

M. PATRICK DUGGAN

M. Patrick Duggan is a writer/cartoonist, and author of several coloring books, including *MYTHS AND MONSTERS Grown-up Coloring Books, Volumes 1-3.*

He has worked as an illustrator, colorist, or writer on several comic books, magazines, and novels–including *Disney Adventures, The Tick, Foodang, The Dark, Green Lantern, Fantastic Four, Clown With A Gun, The Lemming, Bunny & Turtle, The Man Named Elinor, NUOS, Atomic Clown, Atomic Men,* and *LA: Heaven and Hell*–and drawn storyboards for The Tick, DinoTrux, Doug, King of the Hill, Astrid Strudelman, and The Wild Thornberries. In addition, he has drawn many merchandising pieces from trading cards to toy cover artwork for major franchises, including Harry Potter, DC Comics Heroes, and more.

M. Patrick is a proud nerd with profound opinions about Art Nouveau, Art Deco, Mythology, Star Wars, Star Trek, Battlestar Galactica, and... yes... The West Wing. Rumor has it the Sorting Hat put him in Hufflepuff. He's not sure what to think about that.

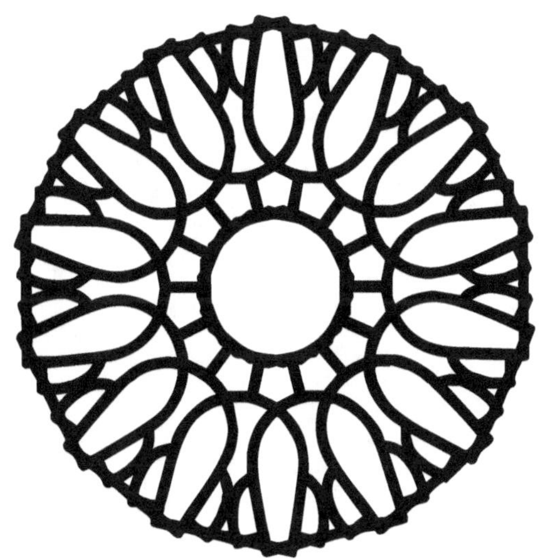

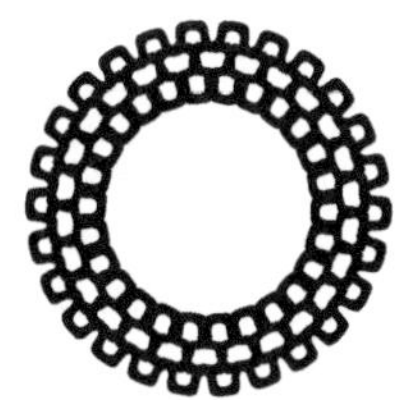

THANK YOU

Writing (and drawing) a book is never really done alone--friends and family are often called-upon for moral (and sometimes financial) support. There are editors, and all kinds of other people involved. To those people, I cannot thank you enough for your endless patience, support, and goodwill. Also, I'd like to include a list of specific people who gave advice and/or extra encouragment (if I forget someone, please forgive me): Alan Pierce, Rachel Fain, John & Virginia Duggan, Joseph Naftali, Alexandrea Weis, Liana Gardner, Dixie De La Tour, Linda Bailey Walsh, Sam Shearon, my Literary Agent Italia Gandolfo, and the support of kind souls/coloring enthusiasts like Ro Ridout and Leslie Hill Allen.

RESOURCES

If you'd like to learn more about Art Nouveau and Adult Coloring Books--here are just a few excellent resources:

ART NOUVEAU
Alphonse Mucha by Sarah Mucha
Gustav Klimt and Egon Schiele by Simon R. Guggenheim Museum
Art Nouveau by Robert Schmutzler
Art Nouveau: The Style of the 1890s by Francesco Abbate
Art Nouveau (The Colour Library of Art) by Martin Battersby

ADULT COLORING BOOKS
coloringbookaddict.com
thecoloringbookclub.com
coloringclub.com
coloringqueen.net
inkspirations.com

www.ingramcontent.com/pod-product-compliance
Lightning Source LLC
LaVergne TN
LVHW081252100826
845148LV00009B/1200

* 9 7 8 0 6 9 2 0 5 0 3 7 8 *